Beloved Wife

A Detective Amy Sadler Mystery: Book Two

Michelle Arnold

ISBN: 1979144230
ISBN-13: 978-1979144230

www.amazon.com/MichelleArnold
facebook.com/MichelleArnoldbooks
twitter.com/berry2120

For Lily, my constant writing companion

ACKNOWLEDGMENTS

Thank you to Claire Highton-Stevenson for letting me bounce off ideas, and Shirley Fisher for never holding back on her opinion. And once again, the medical details in this book would not have made much sense without the help of Kelly Daniel and Linda Pietrzak!

Prologue

She wasn't sure what woke her up at first. She thought it was just because she had to use the bathroom, but something felt wrong. She reached for her favorite teddy bear as she tumbled out of bed and padded towards the door.

When she saw what was in the hallway, her bladder emptied itself of its own accord.

The carpet was covered in flames, and they were licking their way up the wall, threatening to come into her room. She could hear the flames crackling, like a campfire, only so much louder. There was no way to get to the bathroom, or across the hall to her brothers' room, let alone down the hall to her parents' room, or downstairs, out of the house.

"Mommy," she tried to yell, but it came out more as a whisper. She clutched her teddy bear more tightly. "Aunt Mandy," she called, her voice a little louder this time, but still not loud enough.

Then she remembered: Daddy was back home! Daddy was a soldier; he could save them. He had just gotten home a few days ago.

"Daddy!" she called, and this time her voice was closer to the right volume. "Daddy! *Daddy! DADDY, HELP!*"

Her dad's voice sounded from somewhere amongst the flames. "I'm coming!"

She took a few steps back, feeling the heat as the flames crept closer. "Daddy, hurry!"

There was a crashing sound and her dad fell into the room, his clothes burning, though he quickly beat the flames out. He was drenched in sweat.

"Where's Mommy?" she asked him.

"She's still asleep. I'll go back for her. We have to hurry." He opened her window and the night breeze came in. The flames roared and leapt higher. She screamed.

"It's okay, baby, but we have to hurry." He picked her up and put her through the window, holding her as far down as he could. She looked down at the backyard below and screamed again.

"Baby, it's okay, you'll just land in the grass. You'll be all right." She felt his grip loosening.

"Daddy, no!" she screamed. He pulled her back up.

"Okay, we'll go together," he promised. She wrapped her arms around his neck and buried her face against his shoulder, still clutching her teddy bear.

She didn't even realize he'd jumped out the window until they hit the ground, rolling. She felt winded, but otherwise unhurt.

"Okay, I have to go back for the others," Daddy told her, carrying her around the house towards the street.

But the flames were leaping out the windows downstairs. She didn't see how he could possibly get back in.

There was a crowd of neighbors gathering across the street. Daddy took her to them and put her down.

"I called 911," someone told him. "The fire department is on its way."

"Good. Watch my daughter," he said. "The others are still in there. I have to go back."

"You can't go back, it isn't safe! Let the firefighters handle it!"

But he went back anyway, just as the fire trucks were pulling up. The sirens were deafening. She covered her ears, feeling someone's hands on her shoulders but not looking up to see who it was.

She couldn't see much of what was going on, but Daddy

came back, and he was crying. She had never seen Daddy cry before. She'd always assumed he couldn't cry, because he was grown up and brave and strong.

"I can't get to them," he sobbed. "There's no way to get back in. The others are still in there."

People comforted him, but they all stayed to watch the house burn. After what seemed like forever, a firefighter came over to talk to Daddy. She couldn't hear everything, but she heard him say "I'm sorry" and something about a possible break-in. This made Daddy cry even harder.

"Someone did this on purpose?" he cried, his voice shrill. "Someone wanted to kill my family?"

And then he picked her up, and it scared her to be that close to him when he was crying, but she hugged him anyway because she thought that must be what he wanted her to do.

"I'm so sorry, baby," he said in her ear. "I tried. I tried."

He didn't say any more, but she knew. As she looked over his shoulder at their burning house, she knew the rest of her family was still in there.

She knew they were all burning up.

Chapter 1

Amy finished making the bed, just the way Lira liked it, and went down to the kitchen with her golden retriever, Henry, following close behind. Her lovely wife was busy making her breakfast tea, because that was what she drank in the mornings instead of coffee. She was such a weirdo, but Amy loved her for it. She took in the beautiful, feminine form of her wife, with her milky skin and her long, auburn hair. She also had dazzling green eyes, but those were currently focused on opening bags of Irish breakfast tea and putting them into her teapot. Amy noticed the snugly-fitting dress she was wearing and gave a low whistle.

"You're looking extra breathtaking today," she remarked, wrapping her arms around Lira from behind.

Lira leaned back against her. "I know you like this dress on me, so I thought I'd wear it today, since it's a special day."

"Mmm." *Holy shit, what's special about today?* Lira turned in her arms and kissed her. *Think! What is today? It's the seventeenth of November, so that means—*"Yes, our six-month anniversary!"

"We've been married half a year now," Lira said happily. "Although technically it's not an *anniversary*, because the word 'anniversary' comes from the Latin '*anniversarius,*' which means 'returning yearly,' and it hasn't been a whole year yet. Anyway, I made us reservations at Katsina's tonight. Maybe before we go, you can change into something that will take *my* breath away?"

"Do I have anything that does that?"

"*Yes.*"

"Well, get it out and I'll wear it. I never look as good as you do though."

"You do to me." Lira turned back to her tea.

Amy smiled. In her mind, Lira was the most beautiful woman in the world and no one else could possibly measure up, but she knew Lira felt the same way about her. The two women did make a striking couple. Amy was the daughter of a black woman and a white man, so her skin was a light brown, and she had wild black curls falling just past her shoulders. Her eyes were hazel, and her features were sharp where Lira's were soft. She could look very feminine when she put in the effort, but on a daily basis, particularly when going to work as a homicide detective, she let her inner tomboy rule the day. Her job required her to be hard, but having Lira's softness to come home to meant the world to her.

Amy scooped some dog food into Henry's dish, noticing that Clea, Lira's beloved Himalayan cat, was already chowing down on her own breakfast. Then she stood and crossed to the refrigerator. "You want an omelet?" she asked Lira.

"Yes, please."

Amy pulled the ingredients out of the well-stocked fridge — very different from when she lived by herself — and started on two omelets: veggie for Lira, ham and cheddar for herself. This was one of her favorite times of day: the quiet mornings before work, on days when they had gotten up early enough not to have to rush, when Lira was busy with her breakfast tea, the pets were nearby, and everything was peaceful. Amy loved to watch Lira when she was concentrating, whether it was in the county morgue, where she worked as a forensic pathologist, or here in the kitchen. She especially loved it when Lira stuck her tongue between her lips while focusing extra hard. Seeing her do it now, as she poured tea into two cups and added just the right amount of milk and sugar, Amy couldn't help but chuckle.

"What's so funny?" Lira asked.

"Nothing, you're just really cute when you stick your tongue out like that."

"I'm not sticking my tongue out!"

"You were, just a second ago. You always do when you're concentrating really hard."

Lira frowned. "I do not!"

Amy laughed. "You obviously don't realize you're doing it, but you do. You even do it when you're fucking me sometimes!"

"Really?" said Lira is dismay.

"Oh, don't start getting self-conscious because I mentioned it," Amy told her. "I think it's adorable, and I would be really sad if

9

you stopped doing it." She flipped the omelets onto plates, turned the stove off, and walked around the counter to plant a kiss on Lira's head. "Now eat your omelet before it gets cold."

Lira smiled at the kiss, picked up the teacups, and sat down at the table with Amy, humming contentedly to herself. Amy watched her reading the newspaper, taking a mental snapshot of the moment, as she often did. She and Lira had experienced plenty of excitement in their time. They'd solved many a difficult murder case together, been on exotic vacations, and even had their dream wedding. But it was the quiet, everyday moments like this that Amy lived for.

Amy sometimes felt like it was reckless to love someone as much as she loved Lira. It made her feel vulnerable. Too much of her own happiness depended not only on Lira's presence, but on her happiness as well. If anything happened to her, Amy would be destroyed, and everyone knew that. She had hoped, in a way, that settling into married life would make her love for Lira a little quieter, that she could feel the sort of calm love for her that she did for her family, but it hadn't worked out that way so far. It only seemed to grow stronger over time, and she couldn't do anything about it. Not only was she incapable of loving Lira any less, but she knew how much Lira depended on that love, and she deserved it so much.

***

The two women drove to work together, as the Geneva County Morgue was right next door to the Brookwood Police Department. The old morgue had once been in some remote part of the county, but when they'd built the new one some 20 years ago, they'd purchased the lot where a neglected building had been torn down next to the Police Department, thinking it would be more convenient for criminal cases. Amy was glad. It did make life a lot easier for her and everyone else in Homicide to be able to just walk next door for autopsies, and Brookwood (population: 102,390) was by far the biggest city in the Midwestern county of Geneva (and, really, the only town big enough to be called a city). It just made sense to have the morgue here. And when she fell in love with one of the pathologists, it started to feel even *more* convenient.

When she got to work, Amy slumped at her desk and immediately did a computer search for flower delivery. She was browsing a local shop that advertised same-day delivery when her partner, Luis Martinez, walked in. Luis was in his thirties, like Amy, a childhood immigrant from Mexico who, unlike some men, didn't have a problem with strong-willed women. He and Amy had clicked ever since she arrived in Homicide, and she now considered him one of her best friends. She trusted him with her life, which was exactly the way it was supposed to be.

"You been fighting with Lira?" he asked, glancing at the screen.

"No, not at all. I'd just forgotten about today being our six-month anniversary, or whatever the hell you call it. I gotta send her something fast so she doesn't notice that I forgot."

Luis chuckled and sat down at his desk. "It's nice to know it isn't only men who forget anniversaries."

"I didn't totally forget; I just failed to plan in advance this time. It's the first time this has happened to me. I think it'll be easier when we only have to celebrate once a year instead of every month. I mean, people don't do monthly things after the first year, right? She's not going to be making a big deal someday that we've been married three hundred forty-six months?"

"Normally I would say no, but you did marry Lira, so it's possible."

Amy groaned. "Why won't they let me send chocolate-covered strawberries for same-day delivery?"

Luis shook his head, amused. "You should have been paying attention to the date yesterday." He started in on his paperwork, which was all either of them had scheduled for that day. It was technically good news, because it meant there weren't any new murder cases, but a day of paperwork was enough to make Amy *want* to commit murder.

"I'm putting an alert in my phone for next month. Three days in advance, just to be safe." She opened her phone's calendar app and saw a reminder for that afternoon. "Crap, I forgot

Hawthorne's kid is coming to see me today. She needs to interview a cop for some sort of school project."

"Why isn't she talking to someone in his unit?"

"They don't have any women. She specifically asked for a *lady* cop."

"And they couldn't find one?"

"*Very* funny. So anyway, I have until school lets out to think of what I'm going to say to her that's honest without sounding completely jaded."

Amy barely knew Officer Hawthorne, as he was relatively new to Brookwood (a transfer from somewhere, she couldn't remember where) and didn't work in her unit, but there had been stories about his tragic past floating around ever since his transfer. She knew he and his daughter were the only survivors of a house fire a decade ago that had claimed the rest of the family. Local authorities believed the fire had been deliberately set, but they had never found the person responsible. The girl would have been five or six at the time. Amy wondered how much she remembered of the fire.

"I heard the new detective is starting this week, but no one seems to know who it is," Luis said as Amy placed her flower order.

"Carlson's replacement?" she asked. Detective Carlson had just retired.

"Yeah. Here comes Miles. Hey, Miles? Did you find out who your new partner's going to be?"

"Yeah," said Detective Miles. "It's Mitch Wright, from Sex Crimes."

Amy felt her face burning. "You've got to be fucking kidding me."

"I know, they didn't really give me much choice in the matter," said Miles. "But I'll give him a chance. Maybe he's learned from his mistakes."

"Just make sure you look out for yourself, man," said Luis. "You can't trust him to have your back."

Amy couldn't believe it. Mitch Wright had been her partner when she used to work in the Sex Crimes Unit, and he had completely dropped the ball while backing her up during a dangerous undercover assignment, in which she was the bait for a serial rapist. He'd been so busy listening to a game on the radio that by the time he realized the danger she was in, she'd already been badly beaten and was about to be raped. He'd found her tied to a bed, naked, in the most humiliating moment of her life. Mitch had arrested the rapist, Daryl Flynn, and had been suspended without pay, but when she found out Mitch would be allowed to continue working in Sex Crimes, she put in for the transfer to Homicide. She'd never dreamed he would follow her.

"I'm gonna talk to Wheeler about this," Amy grumbled. She pushed herself up from her desk and stormed into Captain Wheeler's office, fuming.

"You're here about Wright's transfer," the older cop said, not looking up from his desk.

"Damn right I am! How did you allow this? You know what that fucker let happen to me when I worked with him. He shouldn't even be in the department anymore, let alone getting a transfer."

Wheeler sighed and took off his reading glasses, looking up at her. "I told Chief Newman my concerns, but he approved the transfer anyway. I don't have the power to stop it. I'll make sure you're not on any assignments with him."

She bit her lip, stymied. She was yelling at the wrong man. The Chief of Police was the one she should be yelling at, although no one in their right mind would. "So why is he here? Why make a transfer at all?"

"My guess is, he was sick of the way people looked at him in Sex Crimes ever since he let you get hurt. I doubt they were sorry to see the back of him."

"Why Homicide? He knows I want nothing to do with him."

He shrugged. "It's more glamourous than Narcotics."

Defeated, she returned to her desk and tried in vain to focus on paperwork.

***

When she got the call from the front desk that afternoon that she had a visitor in the lobby, she was more than happy to abandon her paperwork and go down to meet Haley Hawthorne. The teenager wasn't quite what she was expecting. Generally when a kid wanted to interview a cop for school, it was because they wanted to be a cop someday, but it was very difficult to imagine Haley in that line of work. She was almost unbearably shy, with her willowy frame folded in on itself and blonde hair falling in her face. She would glance nervously at Amy with her big brown eyes (well, one of them; the other was hidden behind her long hair) and then look away quickly as if she had done something wrong. Amy tried to chat with her on the elevator ride to the third floor, but her questions were met with single-word answers.

When she arrived in the squad room with her charge, she was surprised to see a large and very colorful bouquet of flowers on Luis's desk.

"Um, is it your anniversary too?" she asked him.

His nervous glance in her direction was similar to Haley's expression. "Turns out they're for you," he said, hastily passing her the card that accompanied the flowers.

"From Lira, right?" She stuffed the card in her pocket. Based on the deep shade of red Luis was turning, she surmised that whatever Lira had written was best not read in front of people.

"Yeah," he said, looking down at his desk.

"So what are you doing reading my card from Lira?"

"After you left, I went to get some more coffee and I came back and there were flowers on my desk. I thought they were for me."

"Who the hell would have been sending *you* flowers?"

"I have a wife!"

"And when has she ever sent you flowers at work?" Amy moved the flowers to her desk, chuckling. Knowing Lira, she'd probably written out in detail what she planned to do to Amy's vagina tonight. Maybe having to read that would teach Luis to check the name on the envelope next time.

She pulled up a chair for Haley and sat down at her desk, watching the girl pull a folder and notebook out of her backpack.

Haley went through a list of standard questions off of a worksheet. They were pretty dry stuff, like, "Why did you decide to become a police officer?" "What do you like most about your job?" "What is the most challenging part of your job?" At the end of the list was a more interesting question that Haley had added herself: "Is it hard to get respect as a female cop?"

Amy liked this question. It meant that Haley was actually at least somewhat interested in the profession, and it explained why she wanted to talk to a woman.

"Sometimes," she admitted. "In the Academy, and when I first started, and again every time I moved to a new unit, I felt like I had to try twice as hard to earn everyone's respect as I would have if I were a man. Every time I made a mistake, showed fear, or failed to catch a suspect, there were people who assumed it was because I was a woman. So I had to learn to be fearless, never make mistakes, never let anyone get away from me. Now I've been in Homicide for three years, and I've pretty much earned my colleagues' respect, but I still run into people in the field who don't take me seriously as a cop because I'm female. Even women, sometimes."

"So how do you get them to take you seriously?"

"Well, the gun helps. But sometimes, I just have to do my job and not worry about what other people think. I can't force people to respect me. I can only control my own actions, so I just have to focus on that." She studied her charge carefully. "So are you thinking about becoming a cop when you grow up?"

Haley nodded. "I want to save people."

Like she couldn't save her family. "Good for you."

"Do you?"

"Do I what?"

"Save a lot of people."

Amy leaned against her desk, pondering the question. She had to admit, when she was Haley's age, she'd had the same vision of what being a cop would be like.

"The thing is," she began carefully, "when you work in Homicide, you never really know how many people you're saving, or who they are. There are situations where you get to an intended murder victim while they're still alive and you're able to protect them, but more often you're just putting away bad guys who might or might not kill again if you didn't. And you hope, when you put them away, that you are saving people's lives in the process. But there's no way of really knowing, most of the time. You just have to believe that you've made the world a slightly safer place." Amy looked up to see Hawthorne coming into the squad room. "Here's your dad," she said, smiling at Haley. Haley began hastily putting her things back in her bag.

"Thanks for helping my girl with her homework, Detective Sadler," he said, smiling at them both. He pulled a dollar out of his pocket and handed it to his daughter. "There's a soda machine down the hall, to the left," he told her. She ran off, and he turned back to Amy. "Secret admirer?" he asked, indicating her flowers.

"Not so secret," she told him, noting the burn that was partially visible on the side of his neck. She could only imagine how many more burns must be hidden under his uniform. Haley, fortunately, appeared to have been spared. "I've been married for six months, as of today," she said.

"I didn't know you were married," he replied. "Who's the lucky guy?"

She reached around the flowers and pulled out the framed wedding picture she kept on her desk, showing her and Lira in the gardens of the Willis Mansion, a local landmark where they'd held both their wedding and the reception.

"Isn't she a forensic pathologist?" he asked.

"Yep, works right next door," she said proudly. "Dr. Lira Ward. She's the best pathologist in the county, not that I'm biased or anything."

"I've never met her, but I think I've seen her around. Heard people talk about her."

"Good things, I'm sure," said Amy sharply. She knew some people talked about Lira's eccentricities behind her back, and she did her best to squash such talk.

"Of course," he said with a wry smile. "Anyway, better go

find my daughter. Thanks again, Sadler!" He took off, passing Lira as she came in, although he didn't seem to notice her. Lira made a beeline for Amy, carrying the box of Belgian chocolates Amy had ordered for her.

"I got the flowers and chocolates you sent me," she said excitedly, as if it were the first time Amy had done such a thing. That was the thing about Lira: no matter how many times you did something for her, she was still just as thrilled as the first time. Nothing ever got old.

"And I got yours," said Amy, motioning towards the bouquet next to her computer. "I haven't read your card yet, but Luis did, and it must have been something good because he's traumatized."

Lira's jaw dropped. "Why would Luis read it?" she asked, glancing towards her wife's partner, who was pretending to be too busy to notice her. "It was only meant for you."

"Yeah, well, the dork thought someone might have sent *him* flowers. I was out of the room, and the delivery person put them on the wrong desk."

Lira sat in the chair Haley had vacated. "Would you like a chocolate?"

Amy took a chocolate. "Maybe you should offer one to Luis too," she teased. Lira started to get up to do exactly that, but Amy pulled her back down. "Kidding," she said.

Lira bit into a chocolate. "So who was that man you were talking to? I didn't recognize him."

"That's Hawthorne. He's a patrol officer. He transferred here after we were married, I think. He's moved around a bit. Sad story, really. He used to be military, and about ten years ago he did a tour in Iraq for like a year or so. His son was born while he was gone. He finally got home, got to meet his son for the first time, and then a few nights later, the house burned down. Arson. He was able to get his little girl out, but his wife, his sister, and his baby all died. And there might have been a third kid, but I can't remember for sure. Anyway, he decided to leave the military and become a cop after that. Probably didn't want to have to be away from his daughter, since he's all she has left."

"That's so sad! Imagine getting your family back and then losing them again almost immediately."

"I know. It sucks. I don't think they ever found out who started the fire, either."

Lira thoughtfully picked up another chocolate. "So, you can read the card now."

Amy took the card out of her pocket and slid it out of the tiny envelope. Lira would have gotten a typewritten card with her flowers since Amy had ordered online, but this card was, of course, written out in Lira's flowing script.

My beautiful Amy-
So far you have given me:
5 years of friendship
2 years of romance
6 months of marriage
And, as of this writing, 514 orgasms.
I look forward to seeing all these numbers rise through the years.
I love you more each day.
-Your Lira

Amy's eyebrows raised. "514? You've been counting?"

Lira shrugged. "I like to quantify things. But I wrote that a few days ago. The number is 517 now."

"I can't wait to see what you do when we break a thousand."

Lira's brow wrinkled. "Well, those are just the ones you've given me. If I add in the ones I've given you—"

"Lira." Amy put her hand over her wife's. "Let's finish this conversation at home."

"Oh. Right."

Amy squeezed her hand. "You're very sweet. And very, very direct."

Lira smiled. "I'd better get back next door. I'll see you in an hour!" She gave Amy a chaste peck on the cheek and hurried off.

Chapter 2

It was still dark when Lira woke up. She wasn't sure what had woken her. She had a panicked feeling as if she'd just escaped a nightmare, but she couldn't recall a dream. Certainly Lira was no stranger to nightmares. She'd had a lot of them over the past year and a half, after going through an extremely traumatic experience. She and Amy had been working on a case in which a man would abduct a woman and hold her for a few months, raping her repeatedly and carving a tally mark in her skin each time, before killing her and taking another. The day after she autopsied the third victim, Lira had been abducted by the same man, who held her for three days and raped her six times before Amy was able to rescue her, killing the man in the process. Lira had come a long way since then, with Amy's support, but she knew the nightmares, like her scars, would always be there.

Absent-mindedly touching the six raised marks on her chest, Lira looked down at her wife. Amy was sound asleep beside her, sprawled on her stomach with her dark curls spread out over her pillow, breathing evenly. They were both naked, as they had been celebrating six months of marriage well into the night. The cat, Clea, was asleep at the foot of the bed, while Henry was out cold in his doggy bed across the room. Lira had fallen asleep feeling blissful. She didn't know what was causing her dread now, but she couldn't escape the feeling that she had missed something, some important detail, and that not finding it was putting Amy at risk somehow.

She wracked her brain. She couldn't think of a logical reason to feel this way. They had both spent the previous day on paperwork. There were no new active murder cases, no impending trials that either of them would have to testify in, no random threats that Lira knew of. It was possible she'd had a dream she couldn't remember. Lira had a lot of dreams about Amy being hurt or in danger because she knew it was a risk in her line of work. She'd been the one to take care of Amy after Daryl Flynn had beaten her bloody, and she had helped save Amy once when a friend of the man who had hurt Lira came after them. Seeing Amy hurt had nearly destroyed Lira, but she would never ask Amy to take a less dangerous job. Being a homicide detective was a big part of who Amy *was*; to ask her to change was to wish a different kind of death on her. Lira had known what she was getting when she married Amy, and she fully accepted the situation. But she was still going to do everything in her power to protect her wife when necessary.

She didn't know what she could do about that right now, though, so she just reached out and gently moved Amy's hair out of her face before leaning down to kiss her forehead.

Amy stirred a little at this. "I'm tired, Lira," she mumbled. "There's no way I can get you to 600 tonight."

Lira broke into a smile. At least she knew what *Amy* was dreaming about. But before she could settle back down beside her and try to snatch a little more sleep, Amy's cell phone began to ring. Lira watched in amusement as her wife blearily patted around on the nightstand for her phone.

"Detective Sadler," she said hoarsely when she'd finally found it. "Okay." She started fumbling around again, and Lira helpfully handed her a pad of paper and pen from her own nightstand. Amy scribbled down an address. "I'll be there as soon as I can," she promised.

Just then, Lira's phone began to ring. She picked it up, not surprised to see that it was her boss, Geneva Country coroner Arthur Myers. "Dr. Ward," she said brightly.

"Good morning Lira," he said, although the sun wasn't up yet. "We have what appears to be a double homicide out in the Dorset Orchards subdivision."

Lira looked at the address Amy had scribbled down, turning on the lamp. "Is it at 3019 Ellington Lane?" she asked, ignoring Amy's groans at having the light on.

"Yes, how did you—"

"I'm married to a homicide detective, remember? I'll just ride out with her." She hung up and smiled at her wife. "Guess we're starting early today."

"Yeah." Amy pushed her tousled hair out of her face and gazed up at Lira. "How do you do that?"

"Do what?"

"Wake up looking the same as you did when you went to bed. I've never even woken up looking human, in my life."

Lira shrugged. "You move around more in your sleep."

Amy wriggled into her robe and started to set off in search of work clothes, but then turned back. "Aren't you getting up?"

Lira sighed. "Yes. I just...I have a bad feeling."

Amy squinted at her. "You look like Lira," she said, "but you don't sound like Lira. You have a *bad feeling*?"

"I woke up with it. I want to tell you to stay home today, but since I don't know what the bad feeling pertains to, I don't really know how to advise you. Maybe you'd be safer at work."

"Okay, this is turning into *Invasion of the Body Snatchers* real fast. *My* wife doesn't just get a 'bad feeling' for no reason and try to plan her day around it."

"Intuition is simply when our brains gather and process information on a subconscious level. There may be a fully logical reason for my bad feeling that I just don't consciously understand yet."

"Oookay. So, what is this bad feeling about?"

"You. I'm worried someone will hurt you."

"Who?"

"I'm not sure."

"Sweetie, you're freaking me out here."

"I'm sorry." Lira climbed out of bed and put on her own robe. "We have a double homicide. Let's get ready to go."

***

Lira was hypervigilant on the way to the crime scene. They had a 25-minute drive, as the murder had taken place in one of the new constructions on the outskirts of Brookwood.

"I hate this neighborhood," said Amy. "All the houses look practically the same."

"The houses look the same in our neighborhood." They lived in a 1914 brick bungalow that Lira had purchased when she was still single. It sat in a line of nearly-identical brick bungalows all built at the same time. They'd all been individualized somewhat over the past century, though, and they were all beautiful, solid houses.

"Yeah, well, at least in our neighborhood, they look *interesting*. These just look like boxes in different shades of blue and beige, with giant garages on the front. The garages are so big it's practically like a garage with an attached house instead of the other way around. And how do they name these subdivisions? Dorset Orchards? What does that even mean? Do you see an orchard anywhere?"

"No," Lira admitted.

"There probably used to be one and they cut it down to build this ugly-ass subdivision. I don't care how many kids we have, Lira. You're never going to get me to move out here."

Lira smiled. "This isn't the neighborhood I was thinking of moving to. I want a bigger house that's still in the Arts and Crafts style like our house, or perhaps a Prairie-style house. I'd *love* to live in something designed by Frank Lloyd Wright, or something similar. My dream neighborhood would be Oak Boulevard. Those old houses are *so* gorgeous."

"Mm. We can maybe work with that." They got out of the car and met Luis in front of the house.

"Hey. I just got here a few minutes ago," he told them. "I had a quick glance at the victims. The way the woman's tied up might remind you of Flynn a little, but I don't think it's similar other than that."

Lira instinctively reached for Amy's hand. Flynn was in prison, but if someone was copying him, that would give her reason to be worried for Amy's safety. It didn't, however, explain why she had a bad feeling before the call even came in.

Amy took a deep breath. "Okay then, let's see it."

Luis led them through the front door. A man, probably late twenties or early thirties, lay on the floor in his pajamas with his throat slit.

"Looks like he might have just answered the door," said

Amy, walking carefully around the body to look at it from all angles. "Except he's not right by the door. It's like he let the person in."

Lira knelt down beside the body. "Rigor's just starting in the face," she observed. "He's been dead about five or six hours."

"A neighbor who was up early noticed the front door was open, came over to check on them, saw his body," Luis explained. "The wife's upstairs."

Lira finished her preliminary examination of the man's body and then followed Amy up to the master bedroom. Here was a completely different picture: the woman was sprawled on the bed, her wrists and ankles tied to the bedframe, with multiple stab wounds to her chest and abdomen. Her mouth hung open in a silent scream. Lira could immediately see the similarity to Flynn: he had always tied his victims to the bed like this before raping them. She knew he had tied Amy this way, and it made her shudder to think about it.

Amy whistled to herself. "Looks like she was the main target," she said. "It takes a lot of rage to stab someone that many times. This was personal."

As Lira examined the body, Amy walked around the room, the wheels in her head turning. "They're in bed. There's someone at the door, husband gets up to see who it is. He lets the killer in, so it has to be someone he knows. The killer takes the husband out quickly, comes upstairs to find his main target, the wife. He must know her as well, because he hates her with a passion. He ties her up, stabs her a zillion times and then goes back out the way he came in, leaving the door open."

Most of that sounded like wild speculation to Lira, but then, she wasn't a detective. She'd learned through the years that Amy was usually right, even if it did sound like she was jumping to conclusions.

"And look at this," said Amy, pointing to a picture frame that was smashed on the floor. Pulling on latex gloves, she waited for a crime scene tech to photograph it and then gingerly picked it up. "It's the couple's wedding picture. He smashed it."

"I'd say maybe it fell in the struggle, but look at this," said Luis from beside the dresser. "More pictures. Look, here's the guy out with friends, and it's untouched. But here's another wedding shot, and the glass is smashed. And look at this one." He picked up a picture of the woman in her wedding gown. The glass was smashed on this too, and the word *LIAR* was scrawled across the photograph in what looked like blood.

"How much do you want to bet that's her blood?" said Amy.

"Do you think this could be connected to Flynn in some way?" Lira asked.

Amy shook her head. "I don't think so, at least not right now. It's not similar enough, and it seems too personal. We need to look into who might have had a beef with the wife. And, of course, we need to know if she was sexually assaulted."

Lira nodded. That would be her grim responsibility. Nevertheless, she didn't see how her sense of foreboding could possibly be connected to this murder, which meant she still had no idea what it was about.

***

"I know that look in your eyes," Amy told Lira as they drove to downtown Brookwood after finishing at the crime scene. "That hypervigilance. I've seen it on you before, and I've seen it in the mirror. I think I know what caused you to have a bad feeling when you woke up."

"What?"

"Honey, it's obviously PTSD-related. Something triggered you. That's all. It's not intuition."

Lira was quiet for a minute. "Just because I have some post-traumatic stress doesn't mean there can't be real danger in the present moment that I am unconsciously picking up on. Intuition is the result of experience."

"I know, sweetie, and I know it's really hard to tell if what you're experiencing is real or if it's just the PTSD. I'm not trying to put down your intuition; it's just that if it was because of something you'd actually seen recently, you'd be able to figure it out, wouldn't you?"

Lira looked down at her hands. "Maybe. But maybe I just haven't figured it out *yet*."

"And maybe you will, but until then, let's not let fear take over, okay? Whatever might have happened to make you nervous, we're safe right now. Everything's fine. I'm here with you, and we're just doing our normal thing. No one's threatening us."

Lira nodded. "You're right. I just can't stand the thought of anything happening to you again. I want to protect you."

"I know. I feel the same way about you. But I try not to let it keep me from enjoying you in the present."

Lira put her hand on Amy's knee. "I love you. And I *always* enjoy you." She looked out at the sunrise, focusing on her breath, and tried to convince herself that the feeling was just the result of lingering PTSD.

But it still wouldn't go away.

Chapter 3

That night, unsurprisingly, Amy dreamed about Flynn. In the dream, it was Lira he had tied to the bed, while Amy was in the corner, her hands and feet bound so she couldn't intervene. He was tearing Lira's clothes off, planning to make Amy watch while he raped her. Lira was crying, but trying to be brave for Amy. Suddenly her eyes met Amy's, and she could see the tortured, haunting look in them, a look she had seen before. Amy's heart seized and she knew she had to do something, anything, to make it stop, even if it got them both killed. Without warning she lunged forward, launching herself at Flynn, planning to bury her teeth in his throat and just start ripping.

"Amy!"

At the sound of Lira's voice, Amy found herself on her knees next to the bed, a throbbing in her kneecaps telling her she'd bruised them pretty badly. Suddenly Lira was beside her, touching her with gentle hands that were nothing like Flynn's.

"Amy, what happened?"

"Just a bad dream," Amy promised, touching Lira's silky hair to ground herself.

"Do you want to talk about it?"

"Not really." What was she going to say? *Oh yes, I dreamed that you, my beloved wife, were about to be raped for, what would it be? The seventh time? Only you were conscious this time, and I was being forced to watch.*

"Let's get you back in bed." Lira helped Amy up and settled her down on her pillow before climbing in beside her. Clea, who must have jumped down when Amy fell, glared at her from across the room. Henry, being deaf, was still asleep. "Are you hurt?"

"No, I'm fine, just bruised my knees a bit. And my dignity. I feel like an ass for falling out of bed at my age."

"It can happen at any age if your dream is vivid enough," Lira assured her. She knelt down and pressed a tender kiss to each kneecap. "Other things can cause it too. Certain pharmaceuticals. Seizures."

"Well, I'm not on pharmaceuticals, and I've never had a seizure." Amy lay still as Lira moved to kiss her face, then planted a series of light kisses along Amy's jawline, her shoulder, down her arm. These kisses weren't seductive; they were meant to be comforting. And they were.

Amy had never known such sweetness before, and she doubted she ever would again.

She gazed at Lira's dark outline, appreciating her beauty even though she could hardly see her. Lira was just so...pure. Unsullied, in spite of everything she'd seen and experienced, though Amy supposed her experiences must have changed her a little. She no longer possessed quite the same innocence she'd had when Amy first met her, and she wasn't as trusting anymore, except with people she knew well. But overall, her nature was the same. She loved without inhibition, found joy in every possible situation, and gave without expecting anything in return. Amy didn't feel worthy of her, but there was no denying that she made Lira happy. Lira looked at her the way you could only look at the person who had made all your dreams come true. The only thing Amy could possibly do was devote her life to trying to be the person Lira already believed she was.

"Do you think you'll be able to get back to sleep? I can make you some tea if you want." Lira was leaning over Amy, smoothing her hair back from her face gently, as though Amy were the most precious thing in the world. Lira's hair was slightly damp from being washed just before bed, which made the smell of her herbal shampoo extra strong. For Amy, the smell could be soothing or arousing, depending on her frame of mind. Right now it was soothing.

"I can sleep if you lay down with me." Amy opened her arms and Lira eagerly fell into them, snuggling up with her front against Amy's right side, her head on Amy's shoulder, and her arm over Amy's stomach. Amy held her tight and kissed the top of her head, inhaling the shampoo smell. "Maybe that was why you had a bad feeling yesterday," she suggested, hoping a joke would help put the dream images out of her mind. "You somehow knew I was going to throw myself out of bed in the middle of the night. So, you can relax now, because the bad thing already happened."

"I don't think this was it," Lira said, her voice muffled. "I would have needed there to be clues in my environment before yesterday that you were going to do that."

"Do you still have the bad feeling?"

"Yes, but it's less intense. I was thinking…maybe it's because of what you told me, about Mitch moving to your unit."

"That makes sense. I can see why you would feel like I was threatened because of that. But of course, Mitch isn't a *physical* threat. He's just going to be a pain in my ass."

"Yeah. Maybe something did just trigger me, something subtle. It's so hard to tell sometimes."

"I know. I've gone through the same thing countless times." She played idly with Lira's hair. "We're quite the pair, aren't we?"

"We *are* both a bit battle-scarred. But we persevere in spite of it, and I'm very proud of us. In some ways, I think it's made us both better people."

"Do you think it's worth it? Our jobs, I mean?"

"Well, not every bad thing that's happened to us has been the result of our jobs. But yes, of course it's worth it. If we didn't do what we do, I wouldn't have you."

"True, but now that you have me, do you ever want to just run away and become lighthouse keepers or something?"

Lira laughed. "The lighthouses are all automated now, except for the Boston Light, and nobody lives there."

"We can build our own freakin' lighthouse then."

Lira lifted her head. "Those people I autopsied today, what where their jobs?"

"He did something at a bank, and she was a nurse."

"Nothing like our jobs, but they still got murdered."

"Yes. I know."

Lira was quiet for a minute. "There are days when I want to run away somewhere. But I love doing what I do, and I love the people I work with. And I love seeing you do what you do, as long as it makes you happy."

"It does." Amy sighed. "Most days I love it. Today I did not."

"Because it reminded you of Flynn?"

Amy shuddered. "Yes. And the whole couple-killing thing just affects me more now that I'm married, I guess."

"At least they weren't killed in front of each other."

"Yeah. So it wasn't a control thing. He clearly just wanted the man out of the way so he could go after his real target."

"Mmm."

Amy realized Lira was falling asleep, so she stopped talking. She held Lira close, reassuring herself that her wife was whole and happy now. She had been hurt, the same way as in that dream, once. The haunting look in Lira's eyes was one Amy had actually seen, and would never forget, however much she might want to. It was a mixture of pain, terror, and bewilderment. It had slain Amy when she saw it, and would no doubt continue to haunt her for the rest of her life. The truth was that no matter how many horrible things you witnessed, and no matter how aware you were that such things could happen to *anyone*, it was still incomprehensible when it actually happened to you, or to someone you loved.

She had gone through a year of therapy to help her understand that what happened to Lira was not her fault, but what the therapist never understood was that Amy *needed* it to be her fault. It needed to be something she could have prevented, needed to be a stupid and horrendous mistake on her part. Because if it wasn't—if there really was no way that she could have protected Lira—then that meant she couldn't protect her now either. It meant she had no reason to believe nothing like that would happen again, and that was the thought that kept her up at night.

***

"Okay, I want to focus on people who knew Ashley," Amy told Luis the next morning, as they were plotting out who they should interview to get more information about their murder victims. "She was clearly the main target, so she's the key to finding out who did this and why. We can talk to her family, but if she was having an affair or something like that, her friends would be more

29

likely to know than her parents would."

"Maybe we should start at the hospital where she worked and see which other nurses she might have confided in," said Luis. "They could tell us maybe if she was having any marital problems, ex problems, anything like that."

Suddenly a cup of coffee appeared on Amy's desk. She looked up to see who had placed it there and her stomach clenched. Mitch.

"What are you doing?" she asked him, trying to keep her voice level.

"It's a café mocha from Eddie's. Your favorite."

"Oh, brother, you're behind the times," said Luis. "She orders the chai latte now. Gotta be healthy now that she's married to a doctor."

"Yeah, it was so nice of you to invite me to the wedding," said Mitch sarcastically, indicating the picture on Amy's desk.

"I wanted to make sure it really was the happiest day of my life," she shot back. "So why did you buy me a coffee?"

"I'm trying to turn over a new leaf. We're going to be working in the same unit again, and I want to leave all our old problems behind, start over fresh."

She looked at him. He'd put on a little weight since they'd worked together, had a few more gray hairs mixed in with the brown. The lines on his face looked a bit deeper, but he still had the same youthful blue eyes, eyes that looked friendly and fun if you didn't know him well. Eyes that made you want to trust him, until you knew better. "I don't think that's going to be possible, Mitch."

"Why not? I've told you a hundred times, I'm sorry for what I did. It was the stupidest mistake of my career. I've learned from it."

"I'm glad you've learned from it, Mitch, but that doesn't mean I have to forgive you for it."

"What you did, man, that would take a lot to forgive," agreed Luis. "This job only works if we know we can trust our partners with our lives. Amy trusted you with hers, and you let her down. People who don't even know you talk about that, Mitch.

People say you got a lot of nerve to stay in this department after what you did."

"Hey, I paid for my mistake," insisted Mitch. "I was suspended without pay, but the department made the decision to keep me on, so I have every right to be here."

"Well, *I'm* still paying for what you did," said Amy sharply, holding out her hand so he could see the scar on her wrist from where she had struggled in vain against the ropes Flynn had bound her with. "Maybe when I stop having nightmares, I'll forgive you."

He looked at her for a minute. "Yeah, it must have hit you hard," he said quietly. "You had a boyfriend when it happened, but apparently it turned you into a lesbian. That's what people say about *you*." He turned and walked back to his desk.

"He's such an ass," Amy muttered.

"People don't really say that about you," Luis assured her.

"I don't care what they say. My wife is still hotter than any of theirs."

Luis chuckled. "All right, let's head over to the hospital, see what we can find out about Ashley Bibler."

Amy gladly got up to follow him. On her way out, she tossed the coffee into the trash.

Chapter 4

Lira was just finishing her autopsy report on the double homicide when Amy walked in. Lira knew she'd been interviewing people connected to the couple all day, and she looked exhausted.

"Amy." Lira smiled warmly. "How did the interviews go?"

Amy shrugged. "As far as anyone knows, neither of them were having an affair, and they had no enemies."

"You'll find something," Lira promised.

"I suppose our killer wasn't kind enough to leave any of himself behind?"

"Not that I have found. He had stamina, though. He stabbed Ashley twenty-seven times. It's actually very exhausting to stab someone that many times."

"And you know this how?"

Lira chose to ignore that. She was used to Amy getting a little snarky when she was tired or frustrated. "No sign of sexual assault."

"Maybe he's impotent," Amy suggested. "And he's *really pissed* about it."

"It is possible that he was seeking sexual release through this form of penetration because he's unable to have intercourse."

"So, could be about rage, could be about sex. Could be someone they knew. Could be Brookwood's next serial killer." Amy leaned wearily against the wall.

"I'll be ready to go home as soon as I wrap up here. How about you?"

Amy rubbed her forehead. "I'm ready now."

"Would you like to order a pizza so we can pick it up on the way home? And then maybe I can help you relax?"

Amy smiled for the first time since getting to work that day. "You really are the best."

Lira smiled back and returned to her report as Amy stepped out in the hall to order the pizza. Lira's inexplicable apprehension was slowly waning, but it had briefly resurfaced this morning when they arrived at work. Saying goodbye to Amy outside made her stomach tighten, as if she were sending Amy off into grave danger just by letting her go into the police station. She supposed that knowing Mitch was going to be in the squad room with her might be triggering enough. She remembered the aftermath of Flynn's attack all too well. She had sat in the hospital with Amy while she was recovering from her beating, which had involved broken ribs and a pneumothorax. She'd also been there with Amy for the nightmares that followed, and she had been just as outraged as Amy was when she learned Mitch wasn't going to lose his job. Knowing Mitch was going to be near Amy every day now was a pretty reasonable trigger, although logically she didn't think it put Amy in any real danger.

After they'd gotten home and enjoyed their pizza, wine (for Lira), and beer (for Amy), Lira led her wife upstairs with the promise of a backrub.

"I really don't know what I did to deserve you," Amy said as she disrobed and stretched out on her stomach on her side of the bed.

"Is that a joke, or you really don't know?" Lira asked, returning from the bathroom in a silk robe, massage oils in her hands.

Amy smiled to see that Lira had also undressed. "Sometimes, I really don't know."

"You love me more, and treat me better, than anyone else ever has," Lira said simply. "You make me happy. That's why you deserve me." She stood at the side of the bed, rubbing sweetly-scented oil on her hands.

Amy shivered in anticipation. "I'm not as thoughtful as you are though."

Lira ran her fingers up Amy's spine. "I think you're very thoughtful." She began to massage Amy's latissimus dorsi, reveling in the feel of her skin. Amy made a small sound of approval.

"You're the one giving the amazing backrub."

Lira climbed onto the bed, straddled Amy's hips, and began working Amy's trapezius with her fingers. "You're the one who needs it right now. And I enjoy doing it." She moved her fingers up to Amy's neck. She could feel her relaxing and knew she'd be losing her words soon, which was good, because her silly "I-don't-deserve-you" talk was not very conducive to proper relaxation.

Amy was quiet for several minutes. "Well, at any rate, I think you're the best thing ever," she murmured at last.

"The feeling is mutual." Lira leaned forwards and planted a trail of kisses down the side of Amy's neck, then ran her tongue back up. She found Amy's pulsing jugular and nibbled and sucked it, feeling the pulse quicken with her arousal. She began moving her lips along her wife's shoulder.

"I'm guessing the innocent backrub portion of the evening is over now?" Amy asked.

"Oh, Amy." Lira rolled off of her and nudged her onto her back. "It was never an *innocent* backrub."

Amy grinned and untied Lira's robe, sliding it off her shoulders. "This is why I love you."

Lira flashed a smile before lowering her body onto Amy's. She began to kiss her, parting Amy's lips with her tongue and sliding her own tongue inside while grinding her hips against Amy's. She slid her hands in between them, alternately kneading Amy's breasts and flicking her nipples with her fingertips. Amy moved her hips in rhythm with Lira's, sliding her hands gently up and down her wife's writhing body.

Lira started working her way downward. She ran her tongue around Amy's right breast several times before sucking the nipple into her mouth, eliciting a moan from Amy. She rolled the nipple between her teeth, very carefully, not wanting to cause any pain. When she was finished she blew gently on the wet nipple, causing goosebumps to raise on Amy's skin. While doing the same to the left breast, she reached a hand down and began circling Amy's clit with deft fingers. Amy threw her head back, hands now stilled on Lira's back, pelvis tilting upwards to request more.

Lira moved downwards and replaced her fingers on Amy's clit with her tongue. Amy moaned, trying to push herself further into Lira's mouth. Lira seized Amy's hips with both hands and licked her clit faster, then slower, then faster again, until she sensed

Amy was close to the edge. Then she withdrew.

"Lira! No!" Amy cried desperately, grabbing at Lira's head as if to pull her back down.

"Don't worry, I'll get you there," Lira said sweetly, wetting two fingers and sliding them inside of her wife, hearing her gasp. She watched Amy's face as she slid her fingers in and out, pressing her clit with her thumb, until Amy closed up around her fingers, crying out and arching her back with her orgasm. Lira smiled to herself. She loved watching Amy's climax whenever she could. She loved seeing those beautiful features in the throes of ecstasy, loved knowing she was doing that to her. She waited while Amy rocked her hips, trying to get every last bit of pleasure. When she finally relaxed, Lira pulled her fingers out and lay down beside her, slowly licking her fingers, making sure Amy saw her do it.

"You are too sexy for words," Amy said, her voice husky. She gazed at Lira for another moment before moving to take her into her arms. She rolled Lira onto her back and lay on top of her, covering her face and neck in kisses before pulling back to look into her eyes. Lira smiled at her eagerly, but suddenly Amy's face changed. She rolled off of Lira as if horrified.

Lira sat up. "Amy? What's wrong?" She looked down at her body, trying to understand what it was about her that had moved Amy from desire to revulsion so quickly.

"I'm sorry, Lira. Something just...popped into my head. Let's try a different position."

"Did I do something wrong?"

"No. It's not you at all. Come here, beautiful girl." She sat up, pulling Lira up with her. Lira was still worried, but she was already so close to coming after seeing Amy's orgasm. She let Amy pull her onto her lap, wrapping her legs around Amy's waist and her arms around her neck. Amy held Lira close and kissed her before sliding her right hand around to squeeze Lira's left breast and sliding her left hand down between Lira's legs. Finding her sufficiently drenched, she slid her fingers inside, causing Lira to grip her tighter. Lira pushed the odd incident out of her mind for the time being and just rode Amy's fingers, wrapping her body as tightly around her wife's as she could.

"Come on, sweet girl," Amy whispered. "You're almost there." The words were enough to send Lira over the edge, throwing her head back while clinging to Amy's muscular shoulders. She stayed wrapped around Amy for a bit, waiting for her breathing to return to normal, and then she slowly disengaged herself and lay back on her pillow.

"My beautiful Lira." Amy leaned down to kiss Lira's face before lying down beside her.

"What happened? Why didn't you want to be on top of me?"

"Don't worry about it. It wasn't you; it was just me being stupid." Amy's eyes were pleading. It was clear she wanted to move on without any further discussion.

"You looked like you suddenly thought I was disgusting or something."

"*Lira*! I could *never* think that about you!"

"What was it, then?"

Amy hesitated, taking Lira's hand and lacing their fingers together. "It was an intrusive thought," she said finally. "You understand those."

Lira nodded. She didn't have them so much anymore, but there had been a time, shortly after her abduction, when she had barely been able to function for all the intrusive thoughts charging into her head.

"It just sort of popped up, and I felt like a bad guy for a second. I know it doesn't make any sense, but it was how I felt. I didn't want to hurt you."

Lira squeezed her hand. "You could never."

"I know." Amy squeezed back and then pulled Lira into her arms. Lira rested her head on Amy's chest, listening to her heartbeat and breathing until the reassuring sound lulled her to sleep.

Chapter 5

Amy put her car in park and looked up at the apartment building she was about to enter near the Geneva University campus. She and Luis had interviewed just about everyone they could think of, trying to figure out who might have hated Joseph and Ashley Bibler enough to murder them, to no avail. But today they had gotten Ashley's phone records and discovered some recent calls from someone they had not yet spoken to: Rachel Lulling, who was not on the list of known friends the family had provided.

"This neighborhood is a lot different from the others we've been to," Amy observed. Most of their interviews had taken place in subdivisions, neighborhoods with a squeaky clean suburban feel, like the one the couple had lived—and died—in. This was an old house, probably quite lovely in its day, that had been converted into apartments. In Amy's childhood this had been a working-class neighborhood, but it had now been claimed by young professionals who wanted to live close to campus without really being on campus.

Luis shook his head. "Nah, I don't think anyone who lives here would run in the same circles as the people we've seen so far."

"So why was she calling Ashley?" Amy checked the address and rang the buzzer for Rachel's apartment. A minute later a young woman appeared at the door. She looked nothing like the lily-white suburbanites they'd interviewed so far on this case. This woman was biracial, with short dreadlocks and a nose ring. Her outfit made her look almost like a character from *Rent*. She did not look thrilled to see them or their badges.

"I don't know who killed Ashley," she said warily.

"That's okay," promised Amy. "We're just trying to piece together the last few weeks of her life, and we saw that you'd called her recently. Can we come in?"

Rachel stepped back to grant them admittance, leading them into her apartment. Amy and Luis sat gingerly on a secondhand couch that reminded Amy of the one she'd had in her own apartment, back in her bachelorette days. Rachel remained standing.

"So how did you know Ashley?" Luis asked.

"She's my ex," Rachel said, a defiant gleam in her eye. "We dated for two years in college."

This was certainly news. "So Ashley was…bisexual?" Amy asked.

"Yeah. Do you have a problem with that, Officer?"

"It's Detective, and actually, my wife's bisexual."

Rachel's expression softened. "Her parents didn't know."

"That would explain why they didn't mention it. So you've kept in touch with Ashley through the years?"

"We were out of touch for a while. I broke up with her because she wouldn't come out to her family. Her sister knew, and some of her close friends knew, but she couldn't bring herself to tell her parents. They're very religious, and she didn't think they'd take it well. Finally I gave her an ultimatum because I was tired of hiding, and she still wouldn't tell them, so I broke it off. I hated to do it. I loved her. But I couldn't keep living a lie, I mean you can't expect to be part of someone's future if they have to keep you a secret from the ones they love most." She paused and licked her lips. "We stayed friends at first. I even told her we could try again if she ever decided to be brave and live her life honestly. But then she started dating Joe, and she joined his church."

"I'm guessing it wasn't a gay-friendly church?"

Rachel shook her head. "She told me we couldn't be friends anymore, that she was committing herself to being a good Christian and I was only bringing her down. Told me she was a heterosexual woman who had fallen to temptation. Suggested I get help."

Amy could see that Rachel was struggling not to cry at the memory. She could only imagine how it felt to be told by the person you loved that your love was a sickness. "So how'd you end up talking to her recently?"

"She contacted me to apologize for the way she treated me before. She'd noticed a lot of bullshit within the church during her years there and realized no one is as perfect as they pretend to be.

She also confessed that her attraction to women had never really gone away, and that she no longer felt it was wrong."

"Was she interested in getting back together with you?" Luis asked.

Rachel shook her head. "She didn't want to cheat on her husband or anything. She just missed me as a friend."

"Was she happy with Joe?"

Rachel pondered that statement. "I don't think married life was all she hoped it would be, but she did care about him. She wasn't talking about leaving."

"Did he know about you?" Amy asked.

"I don't think he knew we were talking again. He wouldn't have approved. He was the one pushing for Ashley to renounce her bisexuality. But yeah, he knew we dated."

"Did anyone else know you two were talking again?"

"Not that I know of. I don't think she would have told anybody who would have disapproved. I mean, she kept me a secret for two years while we were in a relationship, so it couldn't be that hard to keep it a secret that we were just talking again. We hadn't even seen each other in person."

"Do you know of anyone who might have had a grudge against Ashley, or who could have been angry with her?"

"No. But there's a lot I don't know about her life with Joe."

***

When they left Rachel's apartment, they still had no idea who had killed the Biblers, but Amy felt they might have gained an important piece of the puzzle by learning about Ashley's secret bisexuality. It might have nothing to do with the murders, but it was the only secret they'd been able to dig up on the couple so far. She would have to go back and talk to people again, see how they reacted.

As she and Luis got into her car, Amy glanced at her phone and saw a voicemail notification. She hit play, smiling when she heard Lira's voice.

"Hi Amy, it's Lira. I just wanted to let you know that I got the test results back on Lucas Griffin, and we're ruling his death an accidental

overdose, so it isn't your case anymore. Also, I went to my gynecologist appointment this morning, and I told her I was thinking of getting pregnant in the near future. She said everything looks good, and she gave me a brochure for an excellent fertility clinic where we can have IVF done. I want you to look at it when we get home — the brochure, that is. Anyway, I hope your day is going well. I'll see you later. I love you!"

Amy smiled as she replaced her phone on its clip and started the car.

"Was that the wife?" Luis asked, noting the smile.

"Yeah. She says Lucas Griffin wasn't murdered. Just an overdose."

"Well, that's one less thing on our plates."

"Yeah. You know what's funny though?"

"What?"

"I've known Lira for five years. We've been best friends most of that time. We've been living together for two years now, and married for over six months. But she still says, "it's Lira" every damn time she leaves me a voicemail, like I'm not going to recognize her voice."

Luis chuckled. "That's our doc."

"I should be insulted," laughed Amy. "What kind of person would I be if I couldn't recognize my own wife's voice?"

"But you're not insulted, because you know her."

"Yep. Liras will be Liras. Nothing you can do."

Amy fell silent on the drive back to the station, contemplating the IVF conversation she would be having with Lira later. It was part of an ongoing conversation and something they were both on board with, but they hadn't worked out all the details yet. Every time Amy thought about having a kid with Lira, her stomach swooped like she was going downhill on a very fast roller coaster. It was both thrilling and terrifying. Amy loved kids, and she knew Lira would be an incredible mother. The idea of putting little Liras into the world was almost unbearably wonderful. But she still had a lot of concerns. What if she wasn't a good mother? Or what if she was, but she turned into *her* mother? How would parenthood change her relationship with Lira? And, worst of all, what if they brought an amazing child into the world, and then something horrible happened to that child? She could hardly stand to see *other* people's kids in danger. She didn't know what she would do if it was her own kid.

She was still pondering all of that when she got back to her desk and saw something that made her blood run cold.

Chapter 6

Lira thought Amy seemed subdued on the way home, and she was afraid to ask why for fear that it had something to do with the conversation they were supposed to have tonight. She didn't know why Amy would be reluctant to discuss having a baby, though. She thought they were on the same page with all of that. It was something they'd talked about off and on since before they were even engaged, and Lira had made it very clear that she didn't *need* children in order to be happy. All she really needed was Amy, and Amy had said pretty much the same thing: Lira was plenty enough to make her happy, but kids might be nice if Lira wanted them. Eventually, they had agreed that they would try for a baby. They had also agreed that two children would be ideal. Lira thought they shouldn't wait too long, since they were already in their mid-thirties, and Amy admitted she was right. She certainly hoped nothing had happened to make Amy change her mind.

When they got home, Lira pulled the fertility clinic brochure out of her purse, gave it to Amy to read, and went into the kitchen to start dinner. She tried to brace herself for the possibility that Amy was going to back out of the whole thing. If she did, Lira would have to accept it, but she had to admit that she'd be disappointed. Once they'd made their decision, she had gotten very excited about their future children, had started reading everything she could find about pregnancy and child-rearing. She realized that she already loved their non-existent children, even without knowing anything about them. She supposed it was true that parents never really loved their children for being who they were; how could you even pretend to, if you loved them before you knew who they would be? But there was something beautiful about that blind, inherent love that parents just gave to their children no matter what. There had been times when she wasn't sure if she was on the receiving end of that, and it made her feel good to know she was capable of giving it anyway.

"It's one of the best fertility clinics in the area," she said tentatively as Amy followed her into the kitchen, silently looking through the brochure. "I actually have some eggs frozen already, at a clinic in New York, but they can be transferred here."

"Wow, you never told me that."

"I did it when I was in med school. It was something a lot of us talked about, since many of us were planning on waiting until at least our thirties to have kids. As your eggs age, their fertility decreases. I didn't know yet if I would want to have kids later, but I worried that I wouldn't be able to do it when the time came, so I decided to freeze a few eggs just in case. Even though they've been frozen for over a decade now, those eggs from my twenties still have a better chance of resulting in a live birth than the ones in my body now."

"So we'd use one of those?"

"Maybe."

"Why only maybe?"

"Because we might decide to use yours."

"Mine? But I thought you would have the baby?"

"I will. It's not safe for you to be out in the field when you're pregnant, at least not late in the pregnancy, and you'd be miserable on desk duty, so it makes sense for me to be the pregnant one. But if we do IVF, it won't matter whose eggs we use."

Amy looked startled. "So you could literally have *my* baby?"

Lira broke into a grin. "It would be kind of awesome, wouldn't it?"

Amy finally cracked a smile. "It kind of would. But I always just thought it would be, you know, your egg. So we could have a kid who's kind of like you."

Lira gave Amy some vegetables to chop and returned to the dough she was rolling. "Your genes might be better than mine, though."

"How can you *possibly* say that? That my genes are better than yours? Look at you! You're the most beautiful human being on the planet, and the smartest, and definitely the nicest. It would be a disservice to the planet not to pass your genes on."

"*That* is a gross exaggeration. I think the world needs a new Sadler more than it needs a new Ward. And I don't even know what recessive genes I could be passing on."

"Just because you don't know who your father is? Look, we can make your mom tell us if you want. We'll tell her we're having a baby, so at this point, we could make an argument that we really *need* to know. But I don't think you have any bad genes to pass on. You're an amazing person in every way, and that is what you're going to pass on to our child. I'm the one we should be worried about. If we use my egg, we could have a kid who skips school all the time like my brother, or a kid who seems really responsible on the surface, but cheats on his wife, like my dad."

Lira smiled. "I'm not worried. I think your family has more good than bad to pass on, and we'll be good role models. And anyway, what I was thinking was that we could use my frozen eggs for the second child, because they'll still be just as good then, but your eggs are better now than they will be in a few years. So I thought we could harvest yours, try to conceive with them, and move on to mine if it doesn't work. And if it does work, we'll still have mine for the next baby."

Amy looked thoughtful. "That actually does make sense," she admitted. "So we could have one kid from one of my eggs, and one from one of yours?"

"Yes, if it all works out. I can carry both of them, unless you decide you want to carry one, or we could use a surrogate if necessary."

"Why would we need a surrogate?"

"I doubt we will, but if I had complications during the first pregnancy, it would be inadvisable to go through a second."

Amy stopped chopping. "Is there something you're not telling me?"

"Well, there is always a slightly elevated risk of certain complications when the mother is over 35."

She started chopping again, more forcefully. "Would these complications be dangerous for you, or for the baby?"

"Potentially both. That's another reason to use your eggs right now, because you are 35, so you're right on the line. That means there's a lower risk of the baby having genetic disorders, and when we use my frozen eggs later, the risk will be even lower. But regardless of the age of the eggs, I have a greater risk of complications during pregnancy and delivery due to my age."

Amy heaved a sigh. "Fine. I'll be the pregnant one then."

"What? Amy, no! We agreed I would do it!"

"I'm not letting you do something that would endanger your health when I have a perfectly good uterus, and I'm two years younger than you. So I'll go on desk duty for a while. It can't be that bad."

Lira knew that was a lie. Amy had done temporary desk duty a few times, and it made her so bored she was completely intolerable to be around. She liked getting out in the field, talking to people and exploring places relevant to whatever case she was working on.

"Amy, it's only a slightly elevated risk, for gestational diabetes and hypertension. Both of which are manageable conditions, and my OBGYN will monitor me for them. I wouldn't volunteer to do it if I didn't feel reasonably confident that I could keep myself, and our child, healthy throughout the pregnancy."

"So, you won't die in childbirth or anything?"

Lira gave her a reassuring smile. "It's extremely unlikely. I might bleed more during the delivery than I would have when I was younger, but I'll be in one of the best hospitals in the country. They'll know how to manage it."

"And you want to be pregnant? It's not just to keep me off desk duty?"

"I want very much to feel our child growing inside of me. At least once. It's okay if you want to do it the next time."

Amy looked back at the brochure. "Fine, I guess you can do it. But let the record show that I was willing. I'm not a wimp."

Lira laughed. "No one thinks you're a wimp, Amy. So you do want to go ahead with this?"

"Yeah, of course. But on one condition."

"What's that?"

Amy heaved a sigh. "I know couples who were really happy before they decided to have a baby, but then when they started trying, it was really difficult and it just took over their lives. It was like they couldn't even enjoy each other anymore; all they could do was be miserable that it was taking so long to have a baby. Then they finally have one, but the joy from their marriage is already gone. I don't want that to be us. I want us to still be happy together while we're trying, even if it takes a long time for it to work. And if it never works, I want us to be happy just being the two of us. You are the most important thing in my life. If I have to give you up to have a child, I don't want one."

"It's up to us to make a point of not letting the process take over our marriage, then. Perhaps we can talk to the clinic about reasonable time frames for conception, and just plan to stop trying and adopt if we don't succeed during that time frame. And if adoption doesn't work out either, we'll still have each other. We're happy now; why wouldn't we be happy if we just stay like this?"

"That is my thinking, but it doesn't work out that way for everyone."

Lira stepped around the counter to kiss Amy. "We're not everyone."

"No, we're not," agreed Amy. "You're always going to be enough for me. But…a baby would be amazing."

"Yes, it would." Lira stepped back and appraised her wife. "So what happened at work today? You seem upset about something."

"You can tell?"

"I can always tell. At first I thought you didn't want to have this conversation, but it's not that, so what is it?"

Amy reached into her blazer pocket. "I got a brochure today too. It was on my desk when I came back from questioning someone, sitting right under our wedding picture." She put the wrinkled brochure on the counter. Lira smoothed it out and read the cover:

GAY MARRIAGE HURTS FAMILIES

"You can read the inside if you want, but it's the same shit

I'm sure you've seen before," Amy told her. "All about how couples like us are ruining society."

"Do you know who put it on your desk?"

Amy shook her head. "No one was around when it happened. Had to be a cop though, because no one else could get to my desk that easily. Pretty much everyone knows I'm married to you."

"Did you check the security camera footage?"

"They only have cameras in the hallways. What would we see, besides a bunch of cops walking around in the place where they work?"

"Did you at least check for fingerprints?"

"Yeah. Found nothing."

"I don't like this." Lira could feel her anxiety flaring back up. "This constitutes a threat. Brookwood PD has a non-discrimination policy that includes sexual orientation. Whoever put this on your desk should be disciplined. Maybe even fired."

"Lira, I'm not going to make that big of a deal out of it. If whoever did it knows he got to me, it'll just be giving him what he wants."

"Amy, you have the right to go to work without being harassed by someone for being who you are. This person is saying that you shouldn't have married me." Lira found herself unexpectedly tearing up. How could anyone say she shouldn't have married Amy?

"It's probably just a one-time thing. Some asshole probably found this brochure somewhere, thought of me, and decided it would be funny to put it on my desk. Probably one of the jerks who boycotted our wedding. Or, more likely, Mitch being a jackass."

"Have you told Captain Wheeler?"

"No. Just Luis knows, because he was there when I found it. Look, I'll mention it to Wheeler if it happens again, but otherwise it would just make matters worse if I throw a fit. Cops give each other a hard time. It's just what they do. If you get all upset about it, especially when you're one of the few women in the department, they just give you an even harder time. It'll be better if I act like it never happened."

"But it *did* upset you."

"Well, *yeah*. They're teasing me for being married to you, which happens to be the thing I'm proudest of." She tucked a strand of Lira's hair behind her ear. "And that's probably what this is really about. They're jealous because the sexiest woman in the world is mine and not theirs. So I'm just not going to let them know I'm upset, and we probably won't hear anything else out of them."

Lira nodded, but she wasn't convinced. Her anxiety about Amy had been linked to work, and now she had a solid reason for it. She couldn't help but suspect this was the start of something bigger.

Chapter 7

Amy couldn't believe how difficult Lira was to get out the door for the annual Brookwood Police Department holiday party. *Lira* was the one who had RSVPed for both of them. She was also the one who dragged Amy to a boutique to buy new dresses for the event. But now, suddenly, she didn't want to go because whoever put that brochure on Amy's desk might be there.

"We told everyone we would be there, Lira," Amy said patiently, sitting on the edge of the bed. Lira was in the bathroom, where she had been starting to get ready and was now getting un-ready after suddenly deciding they shouldn't go.

"Tell them you aren't feeling well."

"Honey, Luis and Stella are going to be there. Luis said Stella's starting to show." Stella was Luis's wife. She was now pregnant with their first child, and Lira had been asking her a lot of questions about it every time they saw her.

"We can invite them to dinner next weekend. We don't have to see them tonight."

Amy heaved a loud sigh. It was time to bring out the big guns. "Fine. I guess I'll have to take back this dress you made me get."

Lira popped back out of the bathroom, one earring in her hand. "Don't take it back! You can wear it another time!"

"When?"

"You can wear it to Christmas dinner."

"Sweetie, you're the only one in the family who gets dressed up for Christmas dinner."

"I really wanted to see you wear it, though. And I was going to put your hair up…"

"Well, tonight was the only occasion I had to wear it. It only makes sense to take it back."

"Amy…" Lira picked up the shiny red dress she'd selected for Amy, looked it over, then looked back at Amy, her face a picture of agony.

"Lira," Amy said gently, "you've been convinced I was in

mortal danger for a few weeks now, and here I am, still alive. No one's even tried to hurt me. I'm pretty sure I can make it through a party full of cops."

"Fine," Lira said reluctantly. "But I'm staying by your side."

Amy studied her with concern. She'd really never seen Lira like this before. "Honey, have you considered making an appointment with Christine to talk about how you've been feeling, see what she says?" Lira had seen a therapist for over a year after her abduction, and when she stopped going regularly, Christine had said that Lira could still call if anything came up or if she otherwise needed to talk.

"I'll call Christine if you call Kendra," Lira replied, gazing at her evenly. Kendra was the therapist Amy had seen after Lira's abduction.

"Why do I need to call Kendra?" Amy didn't know why she asked. She already knew. She had been thinking the same thing herself.

"Because you're still acting weird during sex sometimes, and you don't want to talk to me about it. So maybe you should talk to her."

"Okay," she said quietly. "Why don't we get through tonight, and then we'll both do what we need to do."

Lira nodded. "I'm sorry, Amy."

"Hey, you don't have anything to be sorry for. Now go put your jewelry back on, and I'll get dressed."

Not surprisingly, they were late to the party.

"What took you ladies so long?" Stella asked when they finally arrived at the table. "We were getting worried about you."

"We're fine," Amy promised. "Lira was just taking forever to get dressed." She and Lira put their coats down and went to get food from the buffet. Upon returning, Amy sat next to her partner, and Lira sat on her other side.

"That man keeps looking at you," Lira grumbled.

Amy followed her gaze across the room to see Hawthorne sitting with his daughter. He was talking and laughing with other cops. Haley was looking down at her cell phone, hair curtaining her face.

"He's not looking at me, Lira."

"He *was*."

"Probably because he recognizes me. And because I'm with the prettiest girl in the room." She leaned over to kiss Lira's cheek.

"All I know is, he'd better keep his eyes off my woman."

Amy sat back to look at her, incredulous. "*Really*, Lira? What are you turning into?"

"You made it!" said Captain Wheeler, passing by their table. "Watch out for Lugosi from Parking Enforcement. He's already trashed."

"Leave him alone, Wheeler," said Amy. "The guy works in Parking Enforcement. He's got to get his kicks where he can."

Wheeler laughed. "That's true." He went off to find his seat, giving Lira a quick, "You look lovely tonight, Doc," on his way.

"Unfortunately, Mitch is also here, and so's Hardy," Luis pointed out.

Amy looked in the direction he was looking. Sure enough, Mitch was chatting with Hardy, the cop he'd been working with – and listening to a game with – the night Amy was beaten.

"They could at least have the decency to avoid each other, maybe at least pretend to blame each other for what happened," Amy grumbled. "They act like they did nothing wrong."

"If they were decent people, they wouldn't have even stayed in Brookwood," Lira insisted. "They would be too ashamed to even show their faces, let alone stick around and harass the very person they hurt."

"You think Mitch is the one who put that brochure on your desk?" Luis asked Amy.

"I dunno," said Amy, looking down at her food. "It was probably just meant as a joke, but he's already on thin ice, so do you really think he'd do that? Make a joke in such poor taste?"

Luis shrugged. "Well he *is* an asshole, and he sounded pissed about not being invited to your wedding."

"Why should he care? He barely even knows Lira, and he knows I'm never going to be friendly with him after what happened."

"Most of the department was there at the wedding though," said Stella. "I wouldn't have invited him either, but it had to sting."

"Well, I promise not to get pissed if I don't get invited to his wedding," Amy said.

"If he can ever find anyone to marry him," said Lira. "I hate that he's in Homicide now, because not only is he near you, but now *I* have to talk to him more often. It's so hard to be professional when I can't help thinking about what he did to my wife."

"I hate it too, Lira," Amy said with a sigh. "But at least neither of us has to rely on him to keep us safe." She looked back across the room. "I'm going to go ask Haley how her school project went over." She turned to Lira with a teasing smile. "If you're okay with me being that close to Hawthorne."

"Can I come with you?" Lira asked.

Amy sighed, standing up. "Come on, then." She took Lira's hand, helping her out of her chair. "Just promise me you're not going to turn into *that* kind of wife."

"*What* kind of wife?"

"The kind that's jealous all the time, even though she *knows* her spouse only has eyes for her, and won't let her spouse go anywhere alone."

"Oh I'm not jealous. I know you would never cheat on me, and certainly not with *him*. I just don't like the way he was looking at you. It was a bit predatory."

"Okay, well, whatever you call it..." Amy put a hand on the small of Lira's back, steering her towards Haley.

"I'm protective. *You're* the same way."

Amy considered that. She didn't know how Hawthorne had been looking at her, but she pretty much glued herself to Lira's side whenever anyone looked at her the wrong way, so she supposed she couldn't complain. "Okay, fair enough," she admitted.

Haley looked up uncertainly from her phone when she sensed people approaching her. "Detective Sadler," she said in surprise.

Amy smiled warmly. "Hi, Haley! I just wanted to see how

your assignment went over with your teacher. Did you get a good grade?"

"Yeah, I got an A," Haley mumbled.

"Good! This is my wife, Dr. Lira Ward." Amy put her arm around Lira's waist.

Lira tore her eyes from Haley's father, who was deep in conversation with his back to them, to smile at Haley and offer her hand. Haley took it, but only with her fingertips, and quickly disengaged.

"You have a wife?" Haley asked Amy, her eyes wide with fascination.

"Yes, and a far better one than I deserve." Amy kissed the side of Lira's head. "She's a forensic pathologist with the Coroner's Office."

"So you do autopsies?" Haley asked her.

Lira looked thrilled that the kid was asking. "Yes, and I run a variety of tests, among other things. Are you interested in science? The human body?"

Haley shook her head. "It's too gross."

Lira's face fell, but just then, Hawthorne himself turned to notice them standing there.

"Detective Sadler!" he exclaimed jovially. "And this must be your...partner?"

"My *wife*, Dr. Ward," said Amy quickly. Why the hell did so many people have trouble accepting that same-sex couples used most of the same terminology as opposite-sex couples?

"Good to meet you, Dr. Ward," he said, holding out his hand. Amy watched in amusement as Lira hesitantly reached to shake his hand.

"We need to get back to our table," Amy said, eager to avoid the awkward conversation that was sure to follow. "It was good to see you both though!" She took Lira's hand and led her back to the table.

"Isn't he the one whose family died in a fire?" Lira asked.

"Yeah, all except him and Haley." They reclaimed their seats and resumed eating (once Lira had used hand sanitizer from her purse and made Amy use it as well).

Amy had been chatting with Luis and Stella for a few minutes when she looked back at Lira and saw her reading an article on her phone. A closer look revealed a picture of a burning house.

"Lira, is that Hawthorne's house? Put that away!" Amy hissed.

"No one can see what I'm looking at except you. I was just curious to know the full story."

Amy glanced around to see if anyone was paying attention. It felt wrong to read an article about someone's personal tragedy while they were in the room, but she had to admit she was curious too. "Well, what's the full story?"

"They were living down in Belleville when it happened, near St. Louis. Hawthorne's sister, Amanda, had been staying with the family to help with the kids while he was in Iraq. He was scheduled to get home on June 20, but he came a few days early to surprise his family. The fire happened on the day he was supposed to arrive, so officials believe he was the target, that whoever set the fire didn't know he'd come home early."

"That makes sense," said Amy, her brain kicking into detective mode as she wondered who would have wanted to kill the man, and his entire family, the second he got back from Iraq.

"It says the fire started downstairs and spread quickly. There was accelerant on the carpet in the living room, on the stairs, and in the second story hallway, and the front door appeared to have been forced open. His sister was sleeping in the living room. His wife Kim was in the master bedroom, and their two sons, three-year-old Cody and six-month-old Austin, were in a room down the hall. They all died in their beds. Hawthorne says he woke up because he heard the fire, went into the hallway to see what was going on, and ran to his kids' rooms even though he had to go through flames. He heard Haley calling for help—she was almost six—so he went into her room first. He received second- and third-degree burns on his torso and arms trying to get in there. He picked her up and climbed out of her window. He was able to hang onto the sill and then drop down onto the grass while holding her, so they weren't hurt from the fall. She wasn't burned, but there was no way to get back in to save the others, although he tried."

"That is a *really* sad story," said Amy.

"It is," agreed Lira. "But there's something odd about it."

"What's that?"

"His wife was found in her bed. Not by the door or the window, like she was trying to get out."

"People don't always wake up when their house is on fire. You know that."

"Yes, but *he* did. Why didn't he wake her up?"

Amy suddenly felt cold. "Maybe he wasn't sure there was anything going on until he went out into the hallway, and by then all he could do was try and get at the kids?"

"Then he should have called out to her, shouldn't he have? Honestly, if I even thought our house *might* be on fire, I would wake you up before I did anything else."

Amy thought it over, trying to envision a scenario in which she might leave a burning house without Lira. She couldn't. "You're right. He should have gotten her up right away so she could get out, and help get the kids out."

"I'm surprised the local police weren't suspicious of that."

"Well, to be fair, they knew more about the case than we do. He may not have done the best thing in the situation, but people don't always think clearly in a crisis."

"But he was in the military. He's trained to think clearly during a crisis."

"That doesn't mean he's perfect."

Amy looked across the room at Hawthorne cheerfully interacting with his coworkers. She noticed Haley peering at her through the curtain of her hair, although she looked away as soon as she saw Amy looking back. She wondered again how much the kid remembered of the fire. Almost six was plenty old enough to remember, but kids that age often blocked out traumatic experiences.

"Hey, let's not start victim blaming just because the guy

looked at me funny," Amy said gently. "We barely know the man."

"I suppose you're right," Lira conceded. "Can I blame Mitch?"

Amy laughed. "You can blame Mitch for anything you like!"

Chapter 8

"What about this guy?" Amy asked. "It says he's a biology major. He has red hair and green eyes. His baby picture is really cute."

"Put his profile in the 'maybe' folder and we'll review it later," Lira told her. They were looking over sperm donor profiles while eating breakfast and sorting them into file folders, depending on how they felt about them. They had to do this at a time when Amy's mother was unlikely to drop by, as she was very anxious to have a new grandchild and might well try to take over the donor-choosing process if she knew it was going on. They hadn't even told her they were planning on starting IVF soon.

"I want one that sort of looks like you," Amy said, "so we can kind of pretend we actually combined our genes."

"Just to be safe, I should probably do a DNA profile on whatever sperm we get to make sure it didn't come from a biological relative of mine. For all I know, the man who fathered me could have fathered children all over the country."

"Would it be so bad if it was a biological relative of yours? Then we really *would* be combining our genes."

"It wouldn't be so bad this time, but the idea was to buy all the sperm so we could hopefully use the same donor for our second child, and we were planning to use *my* egg that time."

"Oh. Yeah, I guess that *would* be gross."

"What about this guy? He's biracial like you, and he's an *artist*."

Amy frowned. "If we use him, the kid won't look anything like you."

"Well, they don't both have to look like me. I want at least one of them to look like *you*."

"Yeah, but if we use him, even the one from your egg might not look that much like you."

"So you want the sperm donor to be white? That doesn't seem fair."

Amy's lips curled into a smile. "This is going to be the

problem with using the same donor for both kids. We're never going to agree because each of us wants a kid that looks like the other."

"I know, but there are a lot of benefits to having a biological sibling."

"This is how you know you married a doctor: when family planning means making sure everyone has a potential bone marrow donor, should they ever need one."

Lira couldn't help chuckling. "It's not just about bone marrow. There are numerous medical situations in which it helps to have blood relatives around, and the child who grows from my egg will have precious few of those. You have lots of family, but I only have my mom."

"So I think we shouldn't use skin color as a determining factor. Let's just pick someone who's nice and healthy, has a cute baby picture, and does something interesting."

Lira held up the one she'd just been talking about. "I like this one. His baby picture reminds me of you, and he's an *artist.*"

Amy smiled. "Put him in the maybe folder then."

Their phones rang, calling them to a new crime scene, so they put the donor profiles away and headed out.

The call took them out to another new construction at the edge of town. They met Luis outside, along with Drake, the responding officer, and the four of them walked in together. In the foyer they were greeted with the sight of a man in his thirties, clad in pajamas and sprawled on his back at the foot of the staircase, throat slit.

"No," groaned Amy. "Is this for real the same guy again?"

"It doesn't look good," said Officer Drake, an experienced cop in his early fifties. "No signs of a break-in. It looks like Joel Martin here answered the door, maybe even let the killer in."

"Just like the last one," said Luis. "Let me guess: the wife has been stabbed to death in her bed."

Drake nodded, motioning up the stairs. "After you."

Lira took the dead man's vitals before following them up. It wasn't her job to speculate about potential serial killings, but she couldn't help thinking that was what it looked like. She went upstairs to find a woman sprawled across her bed, hands and feet tied, multiple stab wounds in her chest. She took her vitals as well and went to find Amy, Luis, and Drake down the hall, stepping carefully over broken glass. The family pictures hanging in the hallway had been smashed. On one wedding picture, the word *LIAR* was scrawled across the woman's face. There were also, Lira realized to her horror, pictures of kids. One picture showed the couple with two small children, and the word *FAKE* was written across all four smiling faces. As with the first crime scene, the words were written in blood. It had been the woman's blood the first time; Lira guessed it would turn out the same way this time around.

"Two more bodies," Amy told her glumly.

Lira glanced through the nearest doorway, catching a glimpse of baseball posters and stuffed animals. "The kids?" she asked reluctantly.

Amy nodded.

Lira steeled herself and went into the room. A little boy was lying in bed, eyes closed as if he were sleeping, throat slit just like his father's.

"His name is Ethan," said Drake, looking at his notes. "Eight years old."

Lira had the overwhelming desire to talk to the little boy, to tell him it would be okay now, that they would find out who did this to him and his family. And she might have, if she'd been alone with him. At least it would have made *her* feel better.

"There's one more," Amy said gently, when Lira was done with Ethan's vitals. She put a hand on Lira's back as they walked across the hall, and Lira wondered if she was also thinking of the child they hoped to create. It was only going to get harder, she realized, to work this kind of case.

In the third bedroom was a little girl in a princess bed, lying still with not a mark on her. She was neatly covered up with her hands folded on her chest, a stuffed unicorn by her head. She looked perfectly peaceful aside from being dead.

"Emma," said Amy, struggling to keep her voice even. "Five

years old."

Lira leaned close to the little girl. "Cyanosis of the face," she said softly. "She may have been asphyxiated."

"We're going to have to completely re-evaluate every theory we've had about this killer," said Amy. "Before we thought it was personal, that he just wanted to get the husband out of the way so he could kill the wife. But here, he took out the whole family. The worst of his rage is still directed at the woman, but he killed the kids too. And in different ways. The way he covered the girl up and put her toy next to her shows remorse. And he didn't want to cut her."

"If he wanted to show mercy, slitting her throat would actually have killed her faster," Lira pointed out.

"Yes, but it would have been a lot uglier. Maybe he didn't want to shed her blood."

Lira reached a gloved hand out and gently touched the little girl's hairline. "She's so tiny."

"I know." Amy sighed. "We'll find the guy who did this though."

Lira smiled up at her. "I know you will."

Lira gave the okay to have the bodies bagged and transported and went downstairs to wait for Amy. She peered into the living room as Amy and Luis were looking around. She could see a Christmas tree standing in front of the window, a few presents already underneath. The pictures on the fireplace had been smashed, just like the ones upstairs. One word was scrawled across the mirror in what appeared to be blood: *LIES*.

"It's the same message as before, but a completely different family," said Amy.

"Well, we're just gonna have to figure out what these two families had in common," Luis resolved.

"Look at this," Amy said, kneeling in front of the fireplace. With a gloved hand, she pointed to the grate, where there were various scorched remnants of what looked like photographic paper.

"So he's been burning pictures?" asked Luis.

"Yeah." Amy turned to the crime scene photographer. "Have you gotten a picture of this yet?"

"No, but I can." He stepped forwards and took several shots of the grate before giving Amy the okay to disturb the pictures. She gingerly lifted the remnants of one photograph, then another, handing them to Luis to inspect as well.

"They're all family pictures," observed Luis.

"Yeah," said Amy. "He burned the family."

***

Both women were quiet for a while after leaving the crime scene. Lira was brooding over the murdered family, the Brookwood Police holiday party, her lingering feeling of dread. Suddenly she made a connection.

"Maybe it wasn't Mitch," she announced, looking urgently at Amy. "Maybe it was *Hawthorne*."

"What was?"

"Remember when I woke up with that ominous feeling? I thought it was because we found out Mitch was moving to Homicide that day, but that's also the day I first saw Hawthorne. Maybe *that* was what gave me a bad feeling."

"Okay, but what was it about him that gave you a bad feeling that day?"

Lira struggled to remember the details of that afternoon. It had been almost a month. "Something about him made me uneasy when I saw him talking to you, but I brushed it off when you said you knew him. It was weird that he walked right by me without saying anything though. When I go into the station, people I don't know say hi to me all the time, because they know *you* and they recognize me from the pictures on your desk. But he said nothing even though he had just been talking to you."

Amy looked thoughtful. "Actually, I think I had just shown him our wedding picture. He asked who my flowers were from."

Lira shuddered. "It's not any of his business who you get flowers from."

"It's a pretty normal question to ask though. I didn't think that was weird, but I thought it was weird that he didn't seem to notice you right after looking at your picture. Maybe he was just lost in his own thoughts or something."

"I wish I could pinpoint exactly what it was in his demeanor that bothered me. At the time I tried to tell myself it was nothing, because I just get nervous around strange men sometimes now, and usually there's no real threat. But I felt the same way at the party, when I saw him looking at you. He didn't just look like someone who recognized a colleague. He looked *too* interested."

"Well, I hardly ever see him, so he'll just have to be interested from a distance."

"I think you should stay away from him at all costs."

"I'll do my best, Lira, but like I said, I hardly see him as it is."

"When his house burned down, he only saved his little girl," Lira said softly. "His wife and sons died, his sister died, but he saved her. She was about the same age as Emma."

"You're not accusing Hawthorne of murdering people, are you?"

"I'm not accusing anyone of anything. I'm just drawing parallels."

"Well, whoever killed this family didn't even save the girl. He killed everyone."

"Yes, but he showed remorse for killing Emma. Not for the others though, not even Ethan. And both families appear to have let the killer in."

"Yes. That's why we think it was someone they knew."

"It might have been. But most people would also let in a police officer with a badge, even if they didn't know him."

Amy shook her head as if trying to dislodge an unpleasant thought. "You realize that I can't question a fellow cop, can't even hint that I might suspect him of anything, unless I have something solid?"

"I know. I'm not asking you to."

Amy pulled the car into a spot in front of the station and put it in park. "I can't even look him up in the system, because everything we look at is monitored."

"Amy." Lira put a calming hand on her wife's arm. "I was

just making a comparison. I'm not asking you to actively investigate one of your colleagues."

"Good. I'm not accusing someone I barely know of some horrible crime just because he looked at me funny once."

"I know, Amy. I'm sorry. I shouldn't have said anything."

"No, don't be sorry. I'm glad you did say something." She bit her lip, frowning.

"Why? What are you thinking?"

"That thing you said about how most people would let a cop in. You're right." She looked at Lira. "If we can't find someone they both knew, that's what we need to look at. Who are people anyone would let in, even if they didn't know them?"

Chapter 9

Kendra clicked open a pen and looked at Amy, who was slumped in a chair with her arms folded. "So what brings you back here?"

Amy ran her fingers through her hair, avoiding Kendra's eyes. "I guess mostly it's a problem I'm having, you know, in bed. With my wife."

"Well, it's safe to speak freely about anything here."

Amy cleared her throat. "We have a pretty healthy sex life, for the most part, but I just—I can't stand to, you know, *dominate* her, at all anymore. And she's noticed, and it bothers her."

"So, this is something you used to do?"

"Not, like, a bondage thing, but I just mean, I could take charge sometimes, you know? I could just tell her to lie back and let me...let me make her feel good. And she wants me to do it sometimes now, but it's hard."

Kendra glanced over her notes. "So when you say you used to, do you mean before your wife's abduction?"

"Well, yes, it was never a problem back then. And after it wasn't always a problem. At first I insisted that she always be in control, but after more time passed, things went back to normal. But then recently, stuff came back up."

"So what's making it difficult for you now?"

"I don't know for sure what made it come up, but there was one night when she was...on her back, and I was on top of her, and I suddenly thought, *this is what he did to her*. And I felt like a monster for wanting what he wanted."

"That's a very interesting statement. Do you really believe you want what he wanted? What do you think he wanted?"

Amy frowned. "Well, he wanted *her*, and so do I."

"I have no doubt that he wanted her, but that doesn't mean he wanted her in the same way you do. While most people assume rapists are after sexual gratification, it's considered to be more a crime of violence. A rapist's primary goal is to take control of another human being, to cause that person pain, suffering, humiliation. It makes them feel powerful. It actually has very little to do with sexual desire."

Amy shuddered. *He wanted to make her suffer.* And she had, although he hadn't lived to see most of it. She had suffered quite a bit, and Amy along with her. Amy still couldn't wrap her head around the idea that anyone, no matter how depraved, could look at sweet, loving Lira and *want* to see her suffer.

"Amy," said Kendra. "Did you hear my question?"

"No, sorry. Could you repeat it?"

"What is it *you* want when you're having sex with your wife?"

Amy leaned her forehead on her hand. "Well, I guess I just want to be close to her. I want to make her feel good, and kind of…worship her, in a sense. And I want to feel good too, of course, but it's…really an honor just to be allowed to touch her. She's amazing."

"So would you say you're primarily motivated by love for her?"

"Of course."

"Which sounds like the complete opposite of what must have motivated the man who assaulted her."

Amy nodded. "Yeah. Well, yeah."

"And what about your wife? Has she given any indication that your actions remind her of being assaulted?"

"Not at all. I mean, she wants me to be there, so it's not similar to her."

"So you have sex with her because she wants you to, and because you love her."

"And because she's hot."

Kendra smiled. "An element of physical attraction is very important in a healthy marriage. And she deserves for you to find her attractive, doesn't she?"

"Definitely."

"And she's happy?"

"Yeah, other than wondering what my problem is lately."

Kendra looked thoughtful. "So is there something else bothering you?"

"It's...convoluted."

"I can handle convoluted."

"Well, it's kind of always beneath the surface. What happened to Lira, I mean. It's still hard to accept that it happened."

"It *is* a very difficult thing to accept."

Amy stared down at her hands, twisting her wedding ring. "It hurts. It hurts more than anything I've ever experienced."

Kendra nodded sympathetically.

"I'm serious. A man once beat me so hard, he broke my ribs and punctured my lung. I couldn't believe how much it hurt." She paused, biting her lip. "But it still didn't hurt as much as what happened to Lira."

"Emotional pain can be much more intense than physical pain, and often seeing the ones we love hurt is more painful than getting hurt ourselves."

"Yeah, and what happened to her is worse than what happened to me." She swallowed. "It was just about the worst thing that could have happened without her dying."

"Why do you say that?"

Amy looked up, incredulous. "Because she was *violated. Repeatedly*. It took her a while to feel like her body was her own again after that. She still struggles with it sometimes. He just hurt her so badly, physically and emotionally. You should have seen the look in her eyes, right after. I think it's gonna bug me for the rest of my life."

She shuddered, trying to figure out how to articulate her feelings about the most heartbreaking experience she'd ever had. The memories came flooding back: Lira's limp form chained to the bed in Nielson's house, bruises all over her and six tally marks carved right into her chest. Lira waking up in her hospital room and telling Amy she felt ruined—an impossibility, of course, because Lira could *never* be ruined, but it was how she felt. Then there was the nurse bringing Lira an ice pack, which Lira wordlessly situated between her legs, avoiding Amy's gaze as she did so. Amy hadn't said anything either, because what was there to say? *Gee, Lira, putting ice on your pussy sounds very uncomfortable. You must really be in agony if you find that soothing.* Amy had felt so helpless, wracked with a pain that felt physical even though it wasn't.

"What happened to Lira is hard to comprehend because that sort of thing isn't meant to happen to anyone," Kendra said gently, noticing the tears slipping down Amy's face.

"It shouldn't happen to anyone," Amy agreed quietly, brushing the tears away. "But Lira is the sweetest, kindest, most loving person in the world." She shifted her position. "That's part of what makes it so hard. It's not just that I love her. It's that she's never hurt anyone. She just wants to help people. She's so generous and trusting, so selfless. She didn't deserve to have to suffer at all, but she suffered *so much*." Amy was shaking now, the same way she had when she found out Lira had been taken. "I know it sounds cheesy, but she's like some kind of earthbound angel. Sometimes I really think she is." She resumed twisting her ring, trying to ground herself. "I could have protected her if I'd just realized she would become his next target."

"Sounds like we're coming back to you blaming yourself for things you can't control. That was a common theme during our regular sessions."

"Yes, but…that's because I *need* to be in control." She licked her lips. "If what happened to her wasn't my fault, if I couldn't have stopped it, then there's no reason to think I can keep other people from hurting her in the future. And I can't live with that."

Kendra nodded. "I understand that. But unfortunately, part of life is accepting that we can't control everything."

"I don't need to control everything. I just need to control this." Amy wiped another tear away. "We're working a case right now where someone murdered two couples, and the children of the second couple. It reminds me a little of Daryl Flynn's attacks. He would tie women to the bed and then rape them. This guy is also tying women to beds, in a similar fashion."

"Ah. So do you think this is what brought everything back up?"

"Could be. But like I said, it's convoluted. None of the victims in this case have been sexually assaulted."

"But the case reminds you of others that did involve sexual assault."

"Yes." Amy sighed. "Lira just handles all of this better than I do."

"It's actually very difficult to determine whether one person handles a situation better than another, since each person handles things differently, and recovery often isn't linear. But even if we could say with certainty that Lira is handling the situation 'better' than you, I might remind you that she was able to start processing her feelings right away after her abduction, while you had to put your own needs on hold for a few months in order to take care of her. I recall you saying that she found a therapist immediately after being released from the hospital, while you didn't come to me until about three months later. And from what you told me, you had spent most of your time taking care of her both physically and emotionally, making sure she was okay. You hadn't taken the time to even wonder if *you* were okay. So if she seems to have moved on faster than you, it's probably because she got a head start."

"Yeah, I guess." Amy looked at the clock. "I gotta go. My lunch break is almost over, and Lira will freak if I don't eat something."

Kendra smiled warmly. "You'd better get going then. But next time you're having sex with your wife, try to focus on why you want it. It'll help you remember you're not a bad guy."

"I'll try."

"And if you need to take a different approach for a while, that's perfectly okay. There's no need to do anything you're not comfortable with. Lira should understand."

"Yeah. She will."

Amy hurried out of the office, but traffic was slow, and she soon realized there was no way she'd have time to pick something up on the way to work. Resigning herself to skipping lunch after all, she headed back to the station and made her way up to the Homicide squad room. There she nearly ran head-on into Mitch, who was looking peeved about something.

"Hey, aren't you on that case with the family that was just killed?" he asked her.

"Yeah, why?"

"Hawthorne was just up here half out of his mind, going on about how it could have been the same guy who killed his family. They weren't even killed the same way, so why would he think that?"

Amy shrugged. "Dunno. Sometimes killers do change their MO."

"Yeah, maybe, but didn't Hawthorne live somewhere else when that happened? Why would the killer follow him here?"

"I guess he could still be after Hawthorne and his daughter. Has he had any attempted break-ins or anything?"

"Why don't you ask him yourself?"

Amy turned around to see Hawthorne getting off the elevator.

"Detective Sadler," he said breathlessly. "I was just talking to your colleague. I heard about the case you're working on, with the family that was killed?"

"Yeah, he said you thought it might be connected to your family. Why do you believe that?"

"I heard someone say that he burned pictures of the family. He burned the family, just like he burned mine."

Amy frowned. "But he didn't *literally* burn them. There were no signs that he even tried to set the house on fire. Plus, we believe this is the same person who killed a couple last month, and there were no burnt pictures at that crime scene. And you lived hours away from here when your family was attacked."

He shook his head. "You don't understand. This man's been following me."

"What do you mean?"

"That's why we've moved so much. Everywhere we go, he finds us. Sometimes it only takes months, sometimes a few years, but he always finds us."

"Have you been getting threats? Any attempted break-ins,

any fires?"

"No, but people die around us. Everywhere we've lived, couples and families start to die. That's when we move again."

This was even weirder than Amy had expected. "Do you have any idea who would have that much of a grudge against you? For someone to follow you around the country like that...you must have *some* idea who would hate you that much."

He shook his head. "It's the same thing I told police ten years ago. I don't have any idea. The only enemies I ever had were the ones I fought in Iraq."

Amy frowned. It was certainly possible that this was a serial killer who was obsessed with the only targets to survive him. Perhaps that was why he changed from fires to more direct killings, so no one would get away in the future? Still, a lot didn't add up.

"Could you send me information about the other killings you mentioned?" she asked him. "I'll look into the possible connection."

"Yes, of course," he said, relief washing over his features. "Thank you so much, Detective Sadler. You're the first detective to take me seriously about this."

"It's my job to chase down any possible leads. I can't guarantee I'll come up with anything, but I'll do my best."

"I understand. I'll send you the information right away." He turned and went back to the elevator.

Amy sighed, heading to her desk. When she got there, she found an insulated lunch tote sitting on top, bearing a note in Lira's hand:

Amy-
I thought you might not get a chance to eat, so I packed you a lunch.
Love, Lira

Amy broke into a grin and opened the tote to see what was inside. The first metal container held spinach salad—gross, but at least she'd included real salad dressing. She picked up the next container expecting to find a quinoa wrap or some other health food, but instead she found (could it be?) a peanut butter and jelly sandwich, cut into triangles! Granted, it was on whole wheat bread instead of white, but it was still pretty close to being what Amy would have made for herself if she'd had the foresight to pack her own lunch. She dug excitedly to see what other wonders Lira had wrought. The third container held grapes—healthy, but still tasty— and the final one held the greatest wonder of all: two chocolate chip cookies.

So this is what it feels like to be well and truly loved, Amy thought.

She bit into the sandwich and pulled out her phone to send a grateful text to Lira:

Eating the lunch you left me. You know I love you more than anything in the universe, right?

A minute later her phone pinged.

I love you more than anything in the universe too! ☺ I hope your session with Kendra went well.

It did. I'll tell you about it tonight.

Amy put her phone back on her belt and woke up her computer. She returned to some research she'd been working on before her break, eating as she worked, feeling like a knot in her chest was coming undone. Whatever happened with this small hiccup in their sex life, she realized, everything was going to be okay. Lira loved her the same regardless, and she loved Lira enough to find a way over any obstacle for her.

She was just starting to really relax when she noticed the wedding picture she kept on her desk was gone.

Chapter 10

Lira sipped her wine, waiting for Amy to come downstairs. It was a Friday night, and they were going to do a bit of a role playing game. Amy's therapist had told her she might need to take a different approach to sex for a while, and Lira thought pretending to be other people for a night might be helpful. Initially Lira had a very elaborate plan going where they would meet at a bar and then go to a hotel, but Amy was unenthusiastic about that, so they scaled back to just a simple game at home. They had tossed around a few ideas before Amy suggested they just do the bar fantasy.

"I like the way we met," she explained, "but sometimes I read stories about lesbians hooking up after meeting in bars, and it's always really hot, and I don't wish that was what we did because what we really did was better, but I just…wonder what it would have been like, is all."

Lira had smiled. "Well, we can always pretend."

So, in an effort to please Amy and distract her from the intrusive thoughts she'd been having during sex, Lira went shopping for a sexy bartender outfit. She found a very tight top that showed plenty of cleavage and had a built-in bra that pushed her breasts up nicely. She wore it with a short skirt and six-inch heels, and that was it. She was looking forward to the moment when Amy found out that there was nothing underneath her skirt.

Amy came into the kitchen wearing a tank top, ripped jeans, and, surprisingly, makeup. She's left her wild curls down, making no effort to tame them. Lira couldn't suppress a grin when she saw her. She looked hot. She looked like someone who was on the prowl, ready to flirt with a bartender and then take her home for the night. And *Lira* got to be that bartender. She felt a thrill of anticipation as she approached her "customer."

"Good evening, ma'am. What can I get for you?"

"I'll have a beer," Amy said awkwardly as she seated herself at the counter. For someone who had plenty of experience with undercover operations, she had a lot of trouble getting into character for these role-playing games. Lira knew she'd be able to draw her in though. She grabbed a beer from the fridge, popped it open, and set it down in front of Amy, keeping the kitchen island between them for now.

"I haven't seen you here before," she remarked. "What brings you here tonight?"

"Well, I just recently came out, so I thought, maybe it's time to dip my toes in the water. You know, meet some women."

Lira smiled, noticing that Amy was looking at her cleavage instead of her face. "What brought you out of the closet at this point in your life?"

"Well, you know, men suck." Amy made a face. "And there's this really cute pathologist at work. I want to ask her out, but I'm afraid I'll disappoint her, you know, in the sack. I was hoping to get some experience first."

Lira thought that was really sweet. Even Amy's fantasies were about her! Although this meant there were actually two Liras in their fantasy parallel universe: one who was a forensic pathologist, and one who worked in a lesbian bar. And if there were two Liras, did that also mean there were two Amys? If so, what did the other Amy do? She decided it was best not to overthink it.

"I'm sure she would want you to learn on her though, even if it means you're not very confident at first," Lira pointed out.

Amy gave her a weird look. "Okay then. In that case, I guess I'll just leave this lesbian bar and not fuck the really hot bartender who's flirting with me."

"Oh, sorry! Pretend I didn't say that! Just…say your last line again."

"I was hoping to get some experience first," Amy said slowly, as if Lira might not have heard her right the first time.

"Well, you've come to the right place." She stepped around the island and gently pushed a strand of Amy's hair behind her ear, but she felt like she'd gotten out of the groove after breaking character a second ago. She had to find a way to get back in. "Tell me about this pathologist."

"Well, she's smart, she's funny, and she's really sweet. I could see myself marrying her someday, although if I do, some jealous creep will probably steal our wedding picture off my desk at work."

"If that happens, I'm sure she'll give you a new one with an even better frame and *nail it to your desk* if she has to."

Amy laughed. "I could see her doing that."

Lira stepped closer to Amy, sliding an arm around her back, positioning herself so that Amy was getting a close eyeful of her cleavage. "When you ask her out, I'm sure she'll say yes."

"How do you know?"

"Because." Lira kissed Amy's neck. "You are." She kissed again, lower. "So." She kissed Amy's shoulder at the base of her neck. "*Sexy*." She moved the strap of Amy's tank top aside and kissed her shoulder.

Amy put down her beer and grabbed Lira's waist with both hands, eyes darkening with desire. "Well you have the finest fucking pair of tits I've ever laid eyes on."

Lira smiled. "Would you like to touch them?" she murmured, her voice barely audible.

"Oh, fuck, yes." Amy pressed her lips to Lira's cleavage, kissing every bit of skin she could access, then licked her way up each breast before dipping her tongue in between them and running it up the center. Lira's breath started coming faster, her hands tangled in Amy's hair as she felt herself sucked into the fantasy, imagining that she was just meeting Amy for the first time and they were already unable to keep their hands off each other. She tilted Amy's head back and kissed her deeply, her tongue feeling for Amy's. She felt Amy's hands slide up to cup her breasts, thumbs teasing her nipples through the fabric of her top. Lira's heart was pounding when she came up for air.

"Maybe we should go someplace...more private," Amy suggested breathlessly.

Lira had given some thought to that in advance. She wanted a new location, which meant the bed was certainly out of the question, and the couch too. Even the kitchen counter had seen some action in the past. She wanted to do something like on TV, when couples went into some broom closet or something and had sex against the wall. They did have a nice storage closet just off the kitchen, and there were brooms in it, and they certainly hadn't even thought about having sex in there before. So, she figured, it would work well for the fantasy, and should certainly spice things up a bit.

"Come on, I'll take you to the back room," she said in her sexiest voice, grabbing Amy's hand and leading her to the closet. The walls were covered in shelves, so she closed the door firmly behind them and leaned back against it, pulling Amy towards her. This was a position they weren't in often, and it gave Amy a chance to be dominant, if she so chose.

They could barely see each other, as the only light available was what little could force its way in through the small, curtained window from the streetlamps outside. This only served to turn Lira on more as Amy put her hands on her waist and resumed kissing her. Lira pressed her entire body up against Amy's and felt Amy's hands move down to the hem of her skirt, then slowly up the back.

"Mmm." Amy pulled her face back a couple inches. "No underwear."

Lira grinned. "Well, you're not the first girl I've brought back here. I get women like you here all the time."

"Mm. I bet you do." Amy kissed her jaw, her neck, still moving her hands under her skirt. "Is your boss okay with you doing this sort of thing at work?"

"Of course! It's good for business."

Amy laughed. "I bet you *are* good for business." She ran her tongue along Lira's shoulder, hands stilled on her hips under the skirt. "Tell me how you want me to touch you."

"Like this." She grabbed Amy's wrist and brought her hand around to the front. "Am I wet?" She already knew the answer to that, as she was dripping onto her thighs, but she wanted to hear Amy say it.

"You're soaked," Amy told her. "*Damn.*"

"I got wet just looking at you," she whispered into Amy's ear.

"So what do I do? Remember, I've never done this before."

Amy gave her a wicked grin.

Lira thought she was going to go nuts if Amy didn't do something soon. "Caress my—" She paused, remembering what Amy always said about her bedroom talk being too textbook, and tried to think about how a bartender who regularly seduces women would refer to her anatomy. "—my pussy."

Amy's eyes widened upon hearing the colloquialism from Lira's mouth. She began to move her fingers gently back and forth along Lira's swollen folds. Lira's hips moved of their own accord, trying to press herself more fully into Amy's hand.

"Stroke my clitoris," Lira breathed. She cried out involuntarily when Amy obliged. She clung to Amy, fighting the urge to just climb her like a tree. "*Faster*." Amy went faster, attentively watching Lira's face, or what she could see of it in the near-darkness of the storage closet. Lira leaned her head back against the door, not sure she could stand it much longer. "Slow down," she gasped when she felt herself getting too close to climax already. "Just do circles around my—my clit...*yes*...like that." She closed her eyes.

"So, you like this?" Amy asked in a low, husky voice, her tone implying she knew perfectly well that she did.

"Yes! I like it, but...I need you...inside of me."

Amy moved her fingers to Lira's entrance. "How many fingers am I supposed to use?"

Lira struggled not to lose her patience. This was Amy's fantasy. She was doing this for Amy.

"When in doubt, start with one," she said evenly. "But on me, use two. *Now*."

Amy chuckled at Lira's impatience and inserted two fingers. "Now what do I do?"

Lira sighed. Amy had *not* been this clueless during their real first time. "You just move them, up and down, in and out...*mm*...harder..."

"Like that?" Amy asked, knowing perfectly well that she was finally doing it right.

"Yes, like that...mmm...and if you curl them towards the

front, you can...stimulate...oh, yes...yes, like that...*Amyyy!*" Amy watched with a devious grin as Lira exploded into orgasm with little warning. Lira leaned her full weight against Amy, who held her up expertly, stroking her hair with her free hand. Slowly she withdrew her fingers, sucked Lira's juices off, and waited for Lira's breathing to even back out.

"I kind of liked having you tell me what to do," she said.

"I noticed," said Lira. "I think I like it better when you don't pretend not to know what you're doing, but..."

"But what?"

"I kind of liked that you were talking more than usual. You have such a sexy voice."

Amy smiled. "How about I take you upstairs, get you out of these clothes, and fuck you again, only this time, we'll just be ourselves? Cause you know, it's fun to play games now and then, but my wildest fantasy ever is being married to you."

Lira met her eyes, smiling brightly. "Mine is being married to you."

***

Two hours later, the bed was a wreck, but Lira could not have been happier. For the first time in weeks, Amy had brought the same intensity into the bedroom that she possessed when chasing down suspects, and she hadn't flinched or held back at all. Now they were both spent, tangled up together on the bed in silence. Amy had a strand of Lira's hair that she kept winding around her fingers, then letting go, then winding up again. She looked lost in thought.

"You were amazing tonight," Lira told her, breaking the silence.

Amy's eyes moved to hers, looking slightly surprised to be pulled from her reverie. "Yeah? Well, you're *always* amazing." She shifted a little, grabbing a blanket and pulling it over them.

Lira snuggled up closer to her wife. "Why didn't you want to go anywhere for our game tonight? We had fun here, but it's more exciting to do things like that when it takes us out of our familiar environment. We could have had sex in a real back room somewhere."

"I just didn't want other people around. Not right now."

"That's perfectly okay, but can I ask why not?"

Amy shrugged. "I guess because someone's already scrutinizing us. I mean, first he puts a pamphlet under our wedding picture, then he steals the damn picture. What the hell is that about? Did he want it for himself, or did he just not want me to have it?" She wrapped her arms more tightly around Lira. "At least here we don't have to worry about anyone judging us."

"I wonder what he *does* want," Lira said thoughtfully. "I haven't gotten any threats of any kind. There's a wedding picture on my desk too, and it hasn't been disturbed."

"Maybe he never has a reason to go over to the morgue. Maybe my desk is handier for him."

"Or maybe it's not really about homophobia. Maybe he's just upset that you're with me instead of him."

"Yeah, so all he has to do is get me to realize that being gay married is a mistake, and once I dump you, I'll definitely marry him. Even though it would be like trading in a Maserati for a damn Pinto."

Lira laughed. "I can't believe you're comparing me to a car."

"It was the first thing that popped into my head." She picked up another strand of Lira's hair and started twirling it again. "Or maybe it's just someone who has a grudge against me. I keep thinking of Mitch. These things happened only after he moved to Homicide. He walks by my desk a dozen times a day. He could easily have dropped that brochure or grabbed my wedding picture without anyone noticing."

"I wouldn't put anything past him."

"I guess I sort of hope it's him, because if it's him he's just messing with me. If it's someone else…then I don't know."

"And you're afraid it's someone else."

"Yeah." Amy hugged her tighter. "I just keep waiting for the other shoe to drop. I don't know what he's going to do next, but I don't think he's done. If it's Mitch he's going to keep bugging me until I give him the reaction he wants, and if it's someone else, then there's no telling what it could escalate into." She heaved a sigh. "Are you really sure I'm worth it? I mean, you could have married a man instead, and not had to worry about societal disapproval."

"I knew what I was getting into when I married you. And you always say we shouldn't let fear control us." She lifted her head up. "You know how happy you make me, right?"

Amy put her hand on Lira's face and tenderly kissed her. "Yeah. I know. I just worry sometimes that I'm making your life harder than it had to be. It took me forever to admit it, but we all know that this, being with another woman, is what I was always meant to do. You could have gone either way though."

Lira put her head back down and laced her fingers through Amy's. "Not really. I think this is what *I* was always meant to do. Being with you, I mean. I think trying to live without you would be harder than anything I could possibly face with you."

Amy didn't say anything else. She just gratefully pressed her lips to Lira's head and settled down to sleep. Lira, on the other hand, lay awake thinking for a while. It was true what she said: she would gladly face anything with Amy, so long as they could be together. But that didn't really stop her from feeling apprehensive about whatever it was they were about to face.

Chapter 11

By early January, Amy was feeling much better about her sex life. Talking to Kendra really *had* helped. And, so far, no one had stolen the new wedding picture from her desk, even though Lira hadn't followed through on her threat to nail it down (she was too afraid of being arrested for damaging Brookwood Police Department property). Meanwhile, they had settled on a sperm donor and had purchased the entire lot that he had donated, so the fertility clinic was now keeping frozen sperm for them alongside Lira's frozen eggs. Soon they'd be adding some of Amy's eggs to the collection, as she was scheduled to start taking follicle-stimulating drugs later that month.

They still had no good leads on who had killed the Biblers and the Martins. Since the only real secret they'd discovered about the Biblers was Ashley's bisexuality, Amy looked into that angle with the Martins too. But while Carol Martin did sponsor the Gay-Straight Alliance at the high school where she worked, she was by all accounts heterosexual, and her support for LGBT students was no secret. There was also no discernible connection between the Martins and the Biblers.

She had looked into Hawthorne's history as well. She now knew every city he'd lived in between Belleville and Brookwood in addition to knowing the story of his house fire inside and out. She did find unsolved murders similar to the ones she was investigating in a few of these cities, but they were sporadic, and they were missing some telltale details. For instance, none of them had words written in blood or family pictures burned in the fireplace, and the women weren't tied to their beds. Still, they did involve men who were killed quickly and women who were stabbed multiple times, and sometimes children were killed as well. It definitely got her attention, but when she asked Hawthorne for more information, he brushed her off and insisted he'd overreacted.

"The murder of my wife, sister, and sons has been eating away at me for a decade," he explained to her. "Sometimes I get desperate to find answers and I see a connection where there isn't one. I'm pretty sure, now that I've given it more thought, that's exactly what I did this time. I'm sorry I made extra work for you."

Captain Wheeler was determined to solve the case before another family could get killed, however, which meant that he denied Amy's leave request when she wanted to go with Lira to a three-day forensic pathology conference in Milwaukee. Lira was a featured speaker, and she had been rehearsing her presentation for weeks. Amy knew she would have been bored stiff at the conference and would essentially have been going as Lira's trophy wife, but damn it, she was proud of her. She wanted to be there to support her, wanted to give Lira someone to focus on so she wouldn't be nervous while she gave her speech. She also kind of wanted the other nerdy pathologists to see that Lira was very taken. But Wheeler wanted her at the office working the case instead, which meant she and Lira were both sentenced to two nights of sleeping in cold beds.

"At least maybe you'll get a lot of work done with me gone," Lira said as she hugged Amy goodbye at the train station.

"Maybe. I think I work better when you're around."

"Now you'll have nothing to focus on but work. Maybe you'll solve the case before I get back!"

"That would be a miracle." Amy hugged Lira tighter. "I don't want to be away from you for three days."

"Me neither." Lira rested her head on Amy's shoulder. "But it'll go quickly. The nights will be the hardest part."

"Yeah. If you can't sleep…"

"I'll text you."

***

Three days and two nights.

It was the same length of time they had been apart when Lira was abducted.

Of course, this was nothing like that. This time Amy knew where Lira was, knew she was all right, knew when she'd come back. This time, she had no aversion to being in her own home. She put in a normal day at work, had dinner with her mom and siblings, then went home to Skype with Lira before spending a restless night with only their pets for company. She woke up the next morning holding Lira's pillow, which was a very poor substitute for Lira herself, and got up to do it all again.

Lira was pretty chipper on Skype that night. She said someone had asked her to sign a copy of the *Journal of Forensic Medicine* that she'd written an article for.

"Wow, you *are* a real celebrity now," Amy told her. She was sitting in bed eating ice cream, her laptop propped up in front of her. "Just don't go getting a big head about it. Remember, I loved you even before you were famous."

"A doctor from Minnesota offered to buy me a drink because he hadn't noticed my wedding rings, so I had to tell him I was married, and then I told him all about you. And I feel bad for it, but I actually kind of enjoyed turning him down, because he was so handsome."

"Hang on. You enjoyed turning him down *because* he was handsome?"

"Well, yes. Because I have that luxury now. Before I might have been afraid to pass up the opportunity, even if I was tired and just wanted to go back to my room, because I might regret not getting to know him. But now, no matter what anyone has to offer, I just turn them all down because I know I have someone even better at home."

"Aww, Lira."

"I wish you could be here, Amy. Then I could show you off to everyone."

"See, I knew I'd just be your trophy wife if I went."

"Would that be so bad?"

"No, I guess not. You're going to be mine at my next high school reunion."

"I look forward to it." Lira smiled sweetly. "You look tired. Maybe I should let you sleep now."

Amy yawned. "I hate to say it, but I think I *should* try to get some sleep. I didn't last night."

"I was afraid you wouldn't. If you still can't, just text me. I'll answer if I'm awake."

Amy smiled. "I'll do that. And just think: tomorrow night you'll be here in this bed, where you belong."

"I can't wait." Lira smiled sadly. "I love you, Amy."

"I love you too, beautiful. More than anything."

After she closed the computer, Amy took her spoon and the empty ice cream container downstairs. She wasn't going to start living like a slob just because Lira was gone for a few days. Then she went back upstairs, changed into a t-shirt and sweatpants, and climbed into the empty bed to try and sleep.

She was almost out when she heard a car door slam outside. It wasn't anything unusual; it just startled her a little. She rolled over, screwed her eyes shut, and then heard the doorbell ring. She sat up, heart pounding. The house was completely dark. No one in their right mind would be ringing the bell at this hour. As she swung her legs over the side of the bed, she heard the sound of a car speeding away. She grabbed her gun from the nightstand, stuffed her phone in the pocket of her sweatpants, and ran downstairs, cracking the front door open while standing behind it.

As she expected, no one was there. There was, however, a leather-bound book on the front porch. Amy picked it up. *A Bible?* she thought. *Someone drove over here at night just to give me a Bible?*

Several thoughts were swirling in her head as she took the Bible inside, locking the door carefully behind her. The first was that the harassment at work was clearly escalating if they were now bringing things to her house instead of just her desk. The second was that it was very stupid to assume that, just because she was married to a woman, she must not own a Bible. Amy still had the little white Bible her grandparents had given her when she was a kid, and Lira had three different translations on a bookshelf in her home library (in the Religion section, because she really was that organized). So the joke was on this creep.

Amy put the Bible on the kitchen counter and turned the light on, noticing immediately that there were things stuck between the pages. Breathing quickly, she got a pair of latex gloves from Lira's medical bag before investigating further, just in case the perp had been careless enough to leave prints this time. She carefully opened to the first page that was marked and gasped to see her own face.

It was the wedding picture from her desk at work, or half of it anyway. It had been torn down the middle, separating Amy from Lira, although they'd been too close together to separate fully. Lira's hand was still resting on Amy's lower back, and Amy's hands weren't there at all, since they had been on Lira's waist when the picture was taken. You could see bits and pieces of Lira's wedding dress along the ragged edge where the picture had been torn. Amy was smiling widely at the camera, enjoying the most important day of her life with the woman she loved in her arms. She carefully lifted out the picture fragment and noticed that a passage of Genesis had been highlighted on the page:

> And Adam gave names to all cattle, and to the fowl of the air, and to every beast of the field; but for Adam there was not found an help meet for him.
> And the Lord God caused a deep sleep to fall upon Adam, and he slept: and he took one of his ribs, and closed up the flesh instead thereof;
> And the rib, which the Lord God had taken from man, made he a woman, and brought her unto the man.
> And Adam said, This is now bone of my bones, and flesh of my flesh: she shall be called Woman, because she was taken out of Man.
> Therefore shall a man leave his father and his mother, and shall cleave unto his wife: and they shall be one flesh.

Amy turned to the other page that was marked, this time in Ephesians. As she expected, Lira's half of the wedding picture was marking this page, although she was not prepared for the fact that Lira's head had been torn off. She didn't like that at all. Reflexively she pulled her phone out of her pocket and dialed Lira. No answer. She hung up before it could go to voicemail and dialed again, reading the highlighted passage as she did so:

Wives, submit yourselves unto your own husbands, as unto the Lord.

For the husband is the head of the wife, even as Christ is the head of the church: and he is the saviour of the body.

Therefore as the church is subject unto Christ, so let the wives be to their own husbands in every thing.

"Amy?" came Lira's sleepy voice on the other end of the line.

"Lira! Honey, are you okay?"

"Yeah. I was asleep. What's wrong?"

"Somebody just drove by the house and left a Bible by the front door, and it has our wedding picture in it. The one that was stolen. Only they ripped us apart, and they tore your head off, and they used the pieces to mark pages that say things about women getting married and submitting to their husbands."

"Did you see the car?"

"No, I only heard it. But Lira, they rang the bell. They wanted to make sure I saw this right away. And they *tore your head off*. Not mine. Just yours. I'm considering this to be a threat against you." Amy was frantically pacing the room, peering out windows to make sure no one was hiding in the bushes.

"It's a threat against both of us." Lira's voice was strained like she was stretching as she spoke, and Amy thought she heard the *click* of a lamp turning on.

"Your room is locked, right?"

"Yes, of course."

"Are there any extra locks on the door? Like a chain or a deadbolt?"

"There's a chain."

"Can you lock it, please?"

"Yes, but Amy, I'm in Wisconsin."

"I know. Maybe I should come get you. I don't like you being so far away when some psycho is making threats against you!"

"No, Amy, listen. *I'm* in Wisconsin. Whoever dropped off that Bible is in Brookwood. *I* should be safe. *You're* the one we need to worry about."

"I have the doors locked. Lira, the bastard *ripped your head off!*"

"Amy, you need to stay calm. Take a deep breath. My head is still firmly attached to my body. I'm far away from whoever made this threat. Now let's talk about how to keep *you* safe. Have you called Luis?"

"No, I just wanted to make sure you were okay." Amy stopped pacing and started riffling through the Bible.

"Okay, well when we're off the phone, call him and let him know what's going on. Maybe he can come stay with you."

"Hang on, I think I found your head."

"My head?"

"Yeah, it's in Corinthians. There's another passage highlighted. It says, 'Know ye not that the unrighteous shall not inherit the kingdom of God? Be not deceived: neither fornicators, nor idolaters, nor adulterers, nor abusers of themselves with mankind.' So the message I'm getting is that he wants me to realize it's horrible to be gay, ditch you, and find a nice husband to boss me around."

"Well, that's obviously not going to happen," muttered Lira.

"As soon as you hang up the phone, I want you to call the front desk and tell them you aren't accepting any visitors. Anyone wants to know what room you're in, they should turn them away, no matter who it is. In fact, they shouldn't even confirm that you're staying there."

"I'm not sure they would anyway, but I can check with them. Amy, I'm more worried about *you*. You need to call Luis tonight, and in the morning you need to talk to Captain Wheeler, or maybe even Chief Newman. The harassment is escalating, and I really don't think it's Mitch or somebody just giving you a hard time. But it has to be someone from work because they were able to get that picture off your desk, and it's probably the same person who left you that brochure."

"Yeah, most likely. I'll tell him. Listen, I'm sorry I woke you up. You should get back to sleep, but I want you to call me right away if anything weird happens, okay? You probably *are* safer there, but I still don't like you being so far away from me when there's something creepy going on."

"I understand, Amy. You try to get some sleep too, okay? And send me a text in the morning, so I know you're all right."

"I will. In the meantime, anyone knocks on your door, don't answer it, okay?"

"I won't."

After Amy hung up with Lira, she called Luis and told him what happened. They decided he didn't need to come over right away, but she felt better knowing he was aware of the situation, just in case something did happen. She spent the rest of the night on the couch with her gun by her side.

Chapter 12

Lira could hardly focus during the last day of her conference. She kept checking her phone for messages from Amy, needing to know she was still okay. She was relieved when it was finally time to board the train back to Brookwood, even more relieved when the train pulled into the station, and positively ecstatic when she saw Amy waiting for her. She ran into Amy's arms and held her close.

"I'm so glad you're okay," she murmured contentedly. "I was so worried about you."

"Me too." Amy kissed her. "I'd rather have you close by when there's a threat."

Lira pulled back. "Did you talk to Chief Newman?"

Amy shook her head. "He was in meetings all day. On the way here I finally got a message from him, saying he's working late in his office if I still need to talk. We could go there now, or I could just take you home. You must be tired."

"I think we should go see him right away. We need to get this taken care of."

"I thought you'd say that."

They walked the few blocks to the police station hand in hand, Lira rolling her suitcase behind her. "I still think we should be looking at Hawthorne," she said, kicking a little piece of packed snow out of her way. "He fits. He was even in the squad room the day your wedding picture went missing."

"Yeah, but I saw him, and he wasn't holding my picture. He didn't even go near my desk."

"Mitch said he'd already come up once while you were gone. Maybe he took it then. No one would question him walking through the squad room. He just has to pretend he's got something to say to one of the detectives. He could have even committed all those murders he told you to look into!"

"I thought of that, Lira, believe me, I did. When murders follow someone around the country, my first thought is that the person in question could be committing the murders. But it doesn't all add up. For one thing, the murders are erratic, and I've gotten hits in the system on similar murders in places Hawthorne has no connection to. Secondly, if he did it, why come to me?"

"I don't know." Lira chewed her lip as they approached the station. "Maybe he wants you to stop him."

"Well if he wants me to stop him, he should just confess everything. That would make things a whole lot easier."

They went inside and walked up together to the Homicide unit, where Amy unlocked a drawer in her desk and removed the offending Bible, which was now in an evidence bag. Then they made their way down to Chief Newman's office. Lira squeezed Amy's hand as she knocked on the door.

"Detective Sadler," he said, opening the door. He had a deep voice reminiscent of James Earl Jones, which gave him an instant air of authority. "And Dr. Ward. Come in. Have a seat." They both sat in front of his desk and waited while he returned to his chair. "What did you want to talk to me about?" he asked.

"Well, I've been receiving some threatening messages that I believe have come from someone within the department," Amy began. "In November, someone put a pamphlet protesting same-sex marriage on my desk, under my wedding picture. A few weeks later, the wedding picture itself was stolen, and last night, someone rang my doorbell at home and left this on my doorstep." She put the evidence bag containing the Bible on his desk. "Inside are the remnants of my stolen wedding picture, marking pages with highlighted passages describing how wives are supposed to submit to their husbands, and how the sexually deviant can't go to Heaven. They ripped our picture in half to separate Lira and me, and they tore her head off."

They both watched as Newman carefully dumped the Bible out of the bag and used a pen to turn the pages. "So you think this came from someone within the department?"

"Yes, sir. They had to be able to come by my desk in the squad room at least twice without anyone noticing."

"Do you have any theories about who it might have been?"

Amy and Lira exchanged a look. "We have one," Lira said

tentatively, "but we don't have any solid evidence."

"And what is this theory?"

"Officer Hawthorne," Amy told him. "He's on the Special Response Team."

"Yes, I know him. Has he said anything to you personally?"

"No," admitted Amy. "I've only spoken to him a few times. I helped his daughter with a homework assignment once, and Lira had sent me flowers that day, which he asked about. He didn't know I was married. I showed him the wedding picture I kept on my desk—the one that was later stolen—and right after that, Lira came upstairs to see me, and he walked right past her like she wasn't there. Immediately after looking at her picture and being told she was my wife."

"While that could be interpreted as rude, it's hardly a threat, Sadler," Newman pointed out.

"I also noticed him giving Amy a peculiar look at the holiday party," Lira added. "It seemed a little predatory to me."

"Is that all?" Newman asked.

"Well, Hawthorne approached me one day to say that he thought the Biblers and the Martins were killed by the same person who killed his family," said Amy hesitantly. "I looked into it and did find some similar murders in other places where Hawthorne has lived in the past, but he was unable to offer any theories as to who might be behind it, and when I tried to ask follow-up questions, he no longer wished to discuss it. I found that situation peculiar."

"Does that have any connection to the harassment you have experienced?" Wheeler asked.

"No, sir. I just wanted to mention it."

"Chief Newman, I am concerned that whoever has been doing this may have an obsession with Amy," Lira explained urgently. "He highlighted Biblical passages describing how a wife is meant to behave towards her husband, as well as the passage about sexual immorality. Because he has targeted her instead of both of us, my fear is that he is operating under the delusion that he can convince her it's wrong to be married to me, and that she should be with him instead. That sort of obsession can turn deadly, as we've seen before."

"While your obsession theory makes sense, Dr. Ward, it doesn't sound like you have any evidence pointing to anyone in particular," Newman said sternly. "If you'd like to file a formal complaint, Sadler, I will certainly look into it, but I'm not going to focus on any particular officer until you come up with something better than mild rudeness or occasional paranoia. This man's family was brutally murdered right after he got back from a tour in Iraq. I'd be paranoid too."

Amy nodded, looking defeated. "I'll fill out an incident report immediately."

"Isn't there anything you can do to protect her?" asked Lira.

"We're doing all we can do at this point, Dr. Ward. While this qualifies as harassment, no actual threats have been made, so we can't waste resources at this point on hiring a protective detail, especially since we know Detective Sadler is fully capable of looking after herself. And as for Officer Hawthorne, you should know that he volunteers at our local LGBT community center."

Lira was dumbfounded. "He does?"

"Yes. I believe he said one of his relatives was gay, and he likes to support the community in her honor. So to say there is no evidence of him having homophobic tendencies is an understatement. There is, in fact, evidence to the contrary."

Amy looked thoroughly embarrassed. "I apologize for making unfounded accusations," she said. "I'll have the incident report on your desk by morning."

Lira didn't say anything to Amy as they walked out through the squad room. She was afraid Amy would be angry with her now, as Lira's suspicions had humiliated her in front of her boss. Lira felt a little ashamed herself. It wasn't like her to accuse someone on so little evidence. She was a woman of science. She didn't believe in drawing conclusions without empirical evidence. So why couldn't she bring herself to let this go?

"Lira," Amy said quietly, once they were on the elevator. "I know you must be onto something, because you said you had a bad feeling and then bad things started happening, but maybe he's right that we should stop looking at Hawthorne."

"Maybe," agreed Lira. "But perhaps you should start looking at The OUTpost."

"Why's that?"

"Your victims so far have been connected to the LGBT community in some way. Ashley Bibler was bisexual, and Carol Martin was straight but ran a Gay-Straight Alliance. Hawthorne is straight but volunteers at an LGBT community center. You're being harassed by an anti-gay cop. I think we've just found a possible connection between the murders and your harassment."

Chapter 13

Captain Wheeler was at the crime scene this time. That was never a good sign.

"This one's a little different. We have a survivor," he told Amy and Lira when they got out of the car. "A little girl, age nine. I think he tried to smother her, like he did the other little girl, but she didn't die."

"Is she conscious?" Lira asked.

He shook his head. "She's on the ambulance now."

"I need to see her." Lira made her way to the ambulance while Amy and Luis followed Captain Wheeler into the house. Paramedics were tending a small blonde girl who lay motionless on the gurney, her face nearly covered with an oxygen mask. One paramedic was starting an IV.

"Dr. Lira Ward, forensic pathologist," Lira said, flashing her ID. "May I take a quick look at the patient?"

"She's not dead," said one EMT defensively, but the other shook his head at her.

"As long as you can work around us," he told her.

She moved around to the head of the gurney, trying not to get in anyone's way, and lifted the girl's eyelids, shining her penlight in each one. "Petechial hemorrhaging," she murmured. "Was she found in her bed?"

"Yes, the pillow was under her head, and she had a doll tucked under her arm," said the male EMT. "Just looked like she was sleeping. Her breathing was very shallow, but it was present."

"He must have thought she was dead." Lira lightly touched the little girl's hair, her heart aching. "I assume the other family members *are* dead?"

"It's just her parents, but yeah. Dad's dead in the foyer. Mom's dead in the bed upstairs. Bloody mess."

Lira carefully slipped on the usual booties before heading into the house. At least there were no other children, she told herself.

"We've been telling people not to open the door in the

middle of the night," she heard Amy complaining as she walked in to see the now-familiar sight of a man in his thirties sprawled on the floor, blood splattered on the floor and wall beside him. His throat was slashed, but he also had cuts on his hands.

"He tried to defend himself," Lira remarked, kneeling to take his vitals.

"Must have figured out something was wrong," said Luis. "Maybe he did hear the warnings, but something convinced him to open the door this time anyway. Doesn't mean he wasn't wary."

"What would have convinced him? Either someone he knew, or a cop," said Amy. "If we'd told people not to open the door even for the police—"

"You know we can't tell people that. What if the police really do need to knock on someone's door in the night, because of a real emergency?" Wheeler pointed out. "Besides, you know the panic we'd create if we told the public a cop might be killing families. We don't have any evidence yet that it's a cop. It's just a theory."

"How's the little girl?" Amy asked Lira.

"It's too soon to say. Clearly he meant to kill her, but he didn't, so that's something."

"Will she wake up? If she does, she can tell us who did this. She can at least tell us if she recognized him, or if he was wearing a police uniform."

"With a near-suffocation, it's hard to predict how soon she'll wake up," Lira said cautiously. "She could wake in a few minutes, or she could be in a coma for weeks. But with oxygen deprivation, there's always a risk of permanent brain damage."

Amy grimaced. "Meaning she might never be able to tell us anything."

"Yes," Lira admitted. "I just feel horrible that she's going to wake to the news that her parents are dead. Where will she go?"

"Hopefully she's got family who can take her in. We're already on it," Wheeler promised.

"Looks like he torched the pictures again," called Luis from the living room. "And there's something else you need to see.

Lira peered cautiously into the living room and drew in her breath. There was broken glass everywhere from the smashed picture frames, and more pictures lay in a pile of ashes in the hearth. On the wall near the fireplace was a verse written in blood:

A prudent man foreseeth the evil, and hideth himself: but the simple pass on, and are punished.

"Look at this," said Amy, picking up a singed picture with a gloved hand. She held it out for Lira to see.

Although the edges had burned away, and the head had burned off the woman in the picture, she could still make out the little girl from the ambulance, standing next to the woman and smiling widely. She was wearing a t-shirt that read: *I LOVE MY GAY AUNT*. In the background she could see some rainbow flags, and the headless woman was wearing a rainbow wristband.

"I bet that's the gay aunt," said Amy. "Looks like they're at a Pride event."

"It doesn't make any sense," said Lira, frowning. "If he hates gay people, why doesn't he kill gay people? Why does he kill families who just *support* gay people?"

"I don't know," said Amy, shaking her head. "There has to be a reason. We just haven't figured it out yet."

Lira went upstairs, easily finding the master bedroom. Here the woman was tied spread-eagled on the bed, covered in knife wounds. Blood was everywhere, and here too there was a verse on the wall:

And ye shall teach them your children, speaking of them when thou sittest in thine house, and when thou walkest by the way, when thou liest down, and when thou risest up.

"Same as before. He also wrote *LIES* on the pictures up here, just like in the other houses," Luis said as the cops arrived upstairs. "But we still can't figure out what he thinks is a lie. We can't find any evidence that any of these couples were unfaithful."

"No, they all seem like good people," said Amy thoughtfully. "And there's such a difference in how he treats the female victims. Little boys get the same treatment as their fathers, but little girls get the exact opposite of their moms. He can't stand to shed a little girl's blood, but the grown women are the ones he attacks most viciously."

"The moms are clearly the targets of his rage," Luis agreed. "These Bible verses are new, though."

Lira exchanged a meaningful look with Amy, but neither of them said anything. Having finished with the mother's vitals, Lira went down the hall to have a quick look at where the child was attacked.

This room, unlike the others, was almost pristine. Nothing had been smashed or knocked over. Even the bed showed no signs of a struggle, although Lira doubted the girl had held still while he put a pillow over her face. He must have put everything back the way it was. There were a few decorative pillows and stuffed animals neatly arranged, and an American Girl doll lay beside the pillow. It looked like any bed a child had just gotten up from. The only thing out of place was the Bible verse written on the wall, not in blood but in red crayon:

Train up a child in the way he should go: and when he is old, he will not depart from it.

"I definitely want to talk to the gay aunt," said Amy when she had come into the room and seen the verse. "Maybe she can give us some insight into who would do this to her family. And I think..." She frowned. "I think we need to find out which of Hawthorne's family members is gay as well."

"Amy," said Lira urgently, finally voicing her thoughts, "This has to be the same person who's harassing you."

Amy nodded. "Now that he's adding in the Bible verses, I think you're right." She turned to the Captain. "Wheeler, I think we just found solid evidence that our killer is a cop."

Chapter 14

The following morning, Amy told Luis and Wheeler the full details of her and Lira's uncomfortable meeting with Chief Newman.

"I have to admit, it took balls to accuse a fellow officer without a shred of evidence," Wheeler said. "But Newman is right. You shouldn't be focused on Hawthorne. Have you looked into any of the cops who were invited to your wedding, but didn't go?"

"Of course," said Amy. "But if they were going to harass me, why not start when they got the wedding invitation? Why wait until now? This whole thing started not long after that day Haley Hawthorne came to interview me, when I told her dad I was married to Lira. He was new here, so he didn't know."

"She's got a point," said Luis. "Whoever is doing this probably would have started when they found out about Amy and Lira, and everyone besides Hawthorne knew about them ages ago."

"So let's talk to him," said Wheeler. "At least rule him out. I wouldn't accuse him of anything, but he did say he thought the killer could be whoever burned his house down, and then he wouldn't explain it any further. I think that's worth getting to the bottom of."

"I wanted to get to the bottom of it when he first mentioned it, but then he clammed up," said Amy, feeling her phone buzz. She looked down and saw a text from Lira.

"I think we should also show pictures of the murder victims around the OUTpost," Luis said. "The killer had to know all three families from somewhere. Little Zoe Stone's aunt is supposed to get to town this afternoon, so we're gonna talk to her then, see if she knows of any connections. She's supposed to take custody, if the little girl recovers."

"She still in a coma?" Wheeler asked.

"Yeah, but they're supposed to tell us when she wakes up so we can talk to her. Hopefully it'll be soon, and there won't be any brain damage. They said the coma might actually help her brain recover, poor little thing."

"I'm gonna go check on Lira," said Amy, standing up. "She says she's not feeling well."

She went out to the hallway and pushed the down button for the elevator. Lira had been feeling just fine at breakfast. Her phone buzzed with another text:

Also, thank you for the flower. Where did you get it from?

Amy frowned. *What flower?* she typed. She pushed the down button four more times, gave up, and sprinted down the stairs, out the door, into the morgue, and straight to Lira's office. She found Lira sitting at her desk, typing on her laptop, a dark crimson rose beside the computer.

"Hey," she said, trying to calm her breath so it didn't sound like she'd just run the whole way. "I didn't give you a flower."

"Oh." Lira stood unsteadily and stepped around the desk. Amy instinctively put a protective arm around her, pulling her close, although she regretted that a little when she caught a whiff of Lira's breath.

"Honey, what'd you do, eat an entire garlic clove?"

Lira frowned. "I haven't eaten anything since breakfast."

"When did you start feeling sick?"

Without warning, Lira violently wrenched herself away from Amy, stepping back quickly. "Amy," she said urgently. "Don't touch me. Don't touch anything. I need an ambulance."

Amy pulled out her phone. "Why? What's going on?"

Lira wordlessly fell to her knees and threw up on the floor.

"*Lira!*" Amy stepped towards her, but Lira held up a warning hand.

"I mean it, Amy, get back. Call 911. Don't touch me." She looked up at Amy, her eyes wild with fear. "Don't touch me. *Don't touch anything.*"

***

It was some time before they were able to let Amy in to see Lira. She had to get her own blood drawn, at Lira's insistence, and once they'd cleared her, she just paced the visitors' lounge for a while, calling her mom to tell her what happened and then calling everyone at work to ask what they'd learned from searching Lira's office, whether they had any suspects, and so on. Her mother rushed to the hospital and tried her best to calm her, but Amy wasn't having it. Finally someone came to get her, and she charged into Lira's room like a bull in a china shop, pausing for a moment as she noticed how many tubes were coming out of her wife. She was hooked up to monitors, an IV, oxygen. She was very pale, but she was conscious, and she smiled at the sight of Amy. Seeing that it wasn't going to be possible to hug her with all the wires and tubes attached to her, Amy settled for planting a kiss on her forehead and taking her hand.

"How are you feeling? Are you going to be okay?" she asked.

"I feel miserable," Lira admitted. "But I'm very lucky."

"Oh yeah. *So* lucky. Do you know how many people wake up each morning, thinking, 'Maybe today will be the day when I finally get rushed to the hospital with arsenic poisoning!' But you're the only person in Brookwood who actually got to do that today!"

Lira gave her a patient look. "I'm extremely lucky, because I was able to identify my symptoms as arsenic poisoning very soon after ingesting it, which made it possible to remove most of the poison from my bloodstream through hemodialysis and chelation therapy. Most people with arsenic poisoning assume they have a stomach virus or food poisoning and don't get the necessary treatment right away. You may have actually saved my life by pointing out the garlic odor. That was how I knew."

Amy's face relaxed a little. "Yeah, well, that's what we do in this relationship, isn't it? We take turns saving each other's lives."

Lira squeezed her hand. "Any idea who did this?"

"Other than the suspicions we already have, no. But they did learn that the arsenic was in your tea, not on the mysterious flower, so you're the only one who was exposed."

"Perhaps the flower was meant as a warning. I did think it was odd that you gave me a rose of that color, because it represents sorrow and grief. They're usually used for funerals, not romance.

But I thought you might not know that, and you're the only one who ever leaves gifts on my desk."

"I never left you a single flower though," Amy said, frowning. "I guess I need to step up my romance game. The person who's trying to fucking *kill you* is being more romantic than I am."

Lira laughed gently. "That isn't true. But if you do leave me a flower in the future, make sure to attach a handwritten note so I know it's safe to touch."

"Will do." Amy reached up with her free hand to stroke Lira's hair. "But seriously, you're going to be all right?"

"They have to keep me for a few days to monitor my kidneys and other organs for damage, but my prognosis at this point is excellent."

"What is this key-whatever therapy you mentioned?"

"Chelation. It binds itself to the arsenic before the arsenic can bind to my enzymes, so I can excrete the poison in my urine. The only problem is that the drug is also toxic, so I have to be monitored for complications from both the poison *and* the antidote."

"And what would those complications be?"

"Primarily heart and kidney problems. But don't panic. I'm going to be fine. Like I said, I was very —"

"Lucky. Yeah, I know."

"We're going to need to postpone our first IVF cycle," Lira said softly. "So I can have time to recover. I'm still expecting to be able to carry our child, though."

Amy blinked back tears. "If there's any question when the time comes, I still have a perfectly good uterus. The most important thing is for you to be healthy."

"In the meantime, what is being done to keep *you* safe?"

"I'm not concerned for my safety right now. You know who *should* be concerned for their safety? The asshole who put arsenic in your tea."

"Amy. You know I'm not their primary target. You're the one who's been receiving threats."

"The most recent of which involved *your* head being ripped

off, not mine. I think he made his intentions clear. And then he followed through, or at least tried."

"He may not be planning to kill you, but if he's obsessed with you, he could certainly hurt you in other ways. The message he has been sending is that you should leave your 'immoral' marriage and enter into a traditional marriage, probably with him. I'm still far more concerned about you than I am about myself."

"Well, you have an officer outside your room, and I'm not leaving your side, so problem solved." She glanced up. "Shit, Chief Newman is here. I guess they *are* taking this seriously."

Lira followed her gaze through the window into the hallway. "Who's that lady with him?"

"I think she's with Internal Affairs. That's good. It means they get that the person who did this is one of our own."

"Detective Sadler," Newman said politely as he came into the room. "Do you mind if we speak to Dr. Ward privately for a moment?"

Amy looked uncertainly at Lira.

"I'll be fine," Lira promised her.

"Are you sure? Because they can't make me leave if you want me here."

"I'm sure. Is Becky in the waiting room?"

"Yeah. She wanted to see you, but I told her to wait."

"Go find her, tell her I'm going to be fine, and get something to eat. Then come back."

"Okay," Amy said reluctantly. She gave Lira a quick kiss and headed back to the visitors' lounge, where her mother was waiting.

Becky Sadler was a pleasant, mellow woman in her late fifties. She had a round, friendly face, dark skin, short hair that she got professionally curled every Friday, and wire-rimmed glasses. She often had her nose buried in a book, which was the case when Amy found her now, though she quickly put it away when she saw her daughter.

"How is Lira? Can I come see her now?" she asked. Becky loved Lira as she loved her own children, something Amy had always appreciated since Lira's only family was a mother she rarely saw.

"She swears she's going to be just fine since we caught it early, but for now she's pretty sick. You can see her as soon as the Chief of Police is done talking to her. For now, she's ordered me to get something to eat."

"That sounds like good advice to me. Come on, I'll get you something in the hospital cafeteria."

Once Amy had eaten as much as she could stomach under the circumstances, she and Becky returned to the ICU, where Chief Newman and the Internal Affairs lady were just leaving Lira's room.

"Sadler, could we speak to you for a moment as well?" he asked.

"Sure," she replied. "Mom, can you tell Lira I'll be there in a few?"

"Of course," said Becky, eagerly going in to see her beloved daughter-in-law. Amy followed Newman and the lady to the empty visitors' lounge.

"I'm sorry, I don't think we've met," said the woman when they got there, extending her hand. "I'm Kathy Rhodes, Internal Affairs."

"Great," said Amy. "That means the department has recognized that this must have been an inside job."

"I wouldn't jump to that conclusion yet," said Newman, "but we would like to rule out anyone from our department before considering other options. While morgue security is focused on monitoring who goes into the autopsy and cold storage rooms, rather than the offices, we are still looking for someone who could have slipped in and out of the building unnoticed. No one working at the morgue recalls seeing anyone who stood out this morning, and Lira states that she drank the poisoned tea after finishing an autopsy and returning to her office. She began drinking the tea prior to starting the autopsy, so someone must have slipped in during that time to put arsenic in the cup. Whoever it was had likely been there before and knew where the security cameras were located. We got a few partial glimpses of someone entering the lobby in that time frame, but we can't even tell if they're male or female."

"A cop would certainly fit the bill," said Amy. "Cops go into the morgue all the time."

"That being said, we need to know where you were between nine and ten-thirty this morning," said Kathy abruptly.

Amy stared at her evenly. "I was in the squad room with my colleagues, working on a case and discussing the harassment I've been experiencing lately, at the hands of one of my colleagues, which has included a direct threat to my wife's safety."

"Easy, Sadler," said Newman. "We don't really think you did this, but you know it's standard to question the spouse."

"I know," said Amy. She also knew she was going to stay on the suspect list for now, whatever he said. "I just want to know what you're going to do to protect her. You *have* to take the threat seriously now."

"We're taking it very seriously. We've got a uniform outside her room, and we're taking all necessary measures. The officer will keep records of who visits her and when, and no one can come in without Lira's permission – or yours, I assume, because I'm sure you'll be sticking close to her."

"So long as I'm allowed," Amy said dryly, eyeing Kathy Rhodes.

"We'll let you know of any updates," said Newman. "In the meantime, if you get any more strange messages or see anything suspicious, I want you to come straight to me."

"Understood," said Amy. Without another word, she hurried back to her wife's side.

Chapter 15

"This is ridiculous." Amy grabbed the call button beside Lira's bed and punched it repeatedly.

"Amy, stop." Lira's hand landed lightly on Amy's wrist.

Amy looked her wife over. Neither of them had slept well the previous night. Amy technically wasn't supposed to spend the night in ICU at all, but she'd made it very clear to the hospital staff that the only way they were going to get her out was in handcuffs. She had to try to sleep in a chair though, because she couldn't possibly sleep on the bed with Lira. Lira was very "plugged-in" at the moment. There was a blood pressure cuff on her left arm that tightened automatically every few minutes, electrodes on her chest to monitor her heart, a nasal cannula on her face, an IV needle in her right arm, and a pulse oximeter on her right index finger. Amy couldn't lie down with her, or even try to hold her, for fear of disrupting something. And she was mad as hell that Lira needed all those things.

Worse still, the hospital staff was clearly doing a terrible job of managing Lira's pain, because she was very weepy.

A nurse finally came into the room and asked what they needed.

"Isn't there anything else you can give her for pain?" Amy demanded testily.

"I've already administered the dosage indicated in the doctor's orders," the nurse told her patiently.

"Then go find the doctor and tell him it isn't enough! Look at her! She can't stop crying, she's obviously in a lot of pain, and you guys aren't doing shit to help her."

"Amy, it's fine," Lira insisted.

"It's *not* fine. You shouldn't be hurting like this. The whole point of being in a hospital is so they can manage your symptoms!"

"I'll speak with the doctor as soon as he's available," the nurse promised before leaving.

"Amy, come sit with me," Lira pleaded. "You're making me dizzy with all that pacing."

"Sorry." Amy took the seat next to the bed and took Lira's hand in hers. "I wish I could be out looking for the person who did this."

"I'm glad you're here with me instead."

"Whoever it was better be glad I'm not allowed on the case. And when they find out who it is, he'd better hope some other cop gets to him before I do."

There was a knock at the door, and Dr. Lawrence, who had been treating Lira, came in. Amy had to admit, he had shown up faster than she was expecting. Lira, however, looked apprehensive.

"Are you here about her pain meds?" Amy asked.

"No," he said hesitantly. "I'm here about her test results."

Amy did *not* like the way he said that. She squeezed Lira's hand.

"The tests we ran this morning showed that Lira has experienced a rapid decline in kidney function over the past 24 hours, to the point that we now consider her to be in kidney failure. Her liver is also showing a decline in function, and her most recent EKG shows myocardial depression."

Amy felt like a weight had been dropped into her stomach. "What does that mean?"

"It means she's in multiple organ failure."

"But how is that possible? Yesterday you said she was going to be okay."

"It appears the poison did more damage than we originally thought. I'm very sorry."

Amy looked at Lira, who had fresh tears rolling down her face, then back at the doctor. "I don't understand. There's something you can do, right?"

He shook his head. "At this stage, the only thing we can do is manage her pain."

"Well you aren't even doing *that* very well!" Amy shouted, standing up. Lira continued to cling to her hand.

Dr. Lawrence sighed, and Amy decided she hated him. "She has a few days at most," he said.

"A few days? There have to be a lot of things you can try in a few days! There has to be *something* that can make her better!"

"I said at most," he told her. "It could only be a matter of hours."

"You still have to try!" Amy stepped towards him, her stance threatening.

"Detective, I can call you a grief counselor if you need one, but right now I have other patients to see. There is nothing else we can do for her right now." He turned to walk away and Amy started to charge after him, but a strangled cry from Lira caused her to turn around just long enough for him to make his escape.

"Lira, you can't possibly believe him, can you?" Amy demanded. "You're not going to die. I won't let that happen."

"I'm sorry," Lira whispered through her tears. "I don't want to do this to you."

"Hey, why are you apologizing?" Amy sat back down and stroked Lira's hair. "*None* of this is your fault."

"I don't want to leave you." Lira began to cry harder, gasping for air between sobs, which Amy didn't think could possibly be good for someone on oxygen.

"Hey, it's okay. Breathe, sweetie." Amy put an arm over Lira and kissed her face. "You're not going anywhere." Lira felt so warm and alive. There was no way she was dying.

"Hi girls!" Becky came strolling into the room, utterly clueless as to how bad the situation had gotten since her last visit. "Lira, baby, you seem upset."

"They're not managing her pain well," said Amy quietly.

"I brought that book you asked for," Becky told Lira, handing her a book of poetry. Amy wondered what the hell made her suddenly want to read poems in the middle of all this.

"Thank you," said Lira, taking the book and wiping her tears away. "Do you happen to have a pen I could borrow?"

"Sure." Becky dug in her purse. "This one writes in purple ink. Is that okay?"

"It's perfectly fine. Thank you, Becky." Lira took the pen and gave her mother-in-law a sweet, sad smile.

"Mom, could I talk to you outside for a minute?" Amy asked

her.

"Of course." Becky followed Amy into the hallway.

"Mom," Amy began uncertainly. "The doctor's saying now that Lira isn't going to make it, that her heart, liver and kidneys are failing. He says she has days at the most, maybe just hours."

Becky gave her the kind of stare that, in Amy's childhood, was usually reserved for things like broken vases. "What do you mean, she's not going to make it?" she demanded. "Yesterday you said she'd be fine!"

"That's what everyone said yesterday! Now they say she's dying, and there isn't anything else they can do. But she can't be. They just don't know Lira. She's strong. She'll find a way to pull through, right?"

Becky's face softened. "I hope so, baby. I sure hope so."

An hour crept by. Amy suddenly didn't care anymore who had poisoned Lira, as long as she would live through it. Lira was calm for a little while, but as the minutes ticked by, she began to seem increasingly frightened and distraught. It terrified Amy. What the hell would be freaking Lira out so much, unless she could actually feel herself getting closer to death? But she *couldn't*. Amy wasn't planning to let her go.

Eventually Lira's terror grew so palpable that Amy decided to stop worrying about the stupid tubes and wires and just pull her wife into her arms. Holding Lira close made her feel better anyway; obviously Lira couldn't go anywhere if she was holding onto her.

"I don't want to leave you," Lira kept mumbling.

"You won't," Amy would reassure her. "I'm keeping you right here with me."

But Lira would not be consoled. After a while she was sobbing so hard she could barely breathe, and Amy reluctantly called a nurse to see if there was anything they could do to calm her.

"I'll administer a sedative," the nurse promised. Lira looked utterly terrified when the nurse injected the drug into her IV, and it made Amy a little uneasy too. What if she went to sleep and never woke up? But if she kept crying this hysterically, her heart might give out from the stress, so what else could they do?

"Don't give up on me," Lira said suddenly when the nurse walked out. "Please." Her eyes began to close of their own accord, but she fought it.

"I won't," said Amy, although she had no idea what Lira meant.

"Say the thing," Lira insisted. "The thing you always say. From when you first told me you loved me."

"I love you," said Amy quickly, fearing Lira would slip away before she could say the whole thing. "I love everything about you. I love you more than anything."

Lira smiled weakly. "I love you more than anything too."

Amy wanted to kiss her then, was suddenly terrified that she would never get another chance, but Lira was already asleep. She slowly lowered her back onto her pillow, made sure all her wires were still attached, and pressed her lips to the sleeping woman's hair. *Please wake up again*, she thought desperately. *Please don't let that be the end. Wake up and talk to me again, even if it's only for a little while.*

Lira's breathing evened out, and the sound was reassuring. She didn't sound like a dying person; just a sleeping person. Becky left to get coffee, and Amy rested her head on the pillow next to Lira's, her arm across Lira's body, feeling her warmth and the rise and fall of her chest. She stared at Lira's beautiful face, unwilling to close her eyes even though she was exhausted. She didn't even move when a nurse came in to check Lira's vital signs.

But then an alarm went off on the heart monitor. The nurse hit some button and seconds later, a voice came over the intercom announcing a code blue. Suddenly the room flooded with doctors and nurses, and one of them was manhandling Amy out of the room.

"Wait!" Amy cried. "That's my wife! I can't leave her!"

"Ma'am, they need to work on her, and you can't be in the way," the person—a nurse, she supposed—told her sternly. She looked through the window into Lira's room, but as she watched, the nurse went back in and pulled the curtain closed around the bed. Amy looked around helplessly and saw her mother coming down the hall with two coffees.

"Mama." Amy ran towards her mother. "Mom, she's coding. Lira's heart stopped."

Becky froze, her mouth hanging open, and then she awkwardly put her arms around her daughter, still holding the coffees. Amy leaned against her, legs turning to jelly.

"Come on, Amy, let's go to the waiting room so you can sit down."

"No, I need to stay here," Amy insisted, looking helplessly towards Lira's room.

"They'll know where to find us. Come on." Becky guided her down the hall to the visitors' lounge and into a chair. Amy slumped over, head in her hands, shaking violently. Her mother rubbed her back reassuringly as they waited in silence for what felt like an eternity. After Amy decided she'd waited long enough, she got up and charged out of the room to see what was going on, running headlong into Dr. Lawrence on the other side of the door.

"Detective," he said quietly. She stared at him, realizing she couldn't find her voice to ask how Lira was. "I'm really sorry," he told her, reaching to pat her hand, and she could feel her heart shattering into a million pieces. She pushed past him and ran back to Lira's room, determined that if she saw and touched her again she could make her be alive. But when she got to the room, Lira wasn't there. Her bed was empty, the blankets in a heap at the bottom, a small dent in the pillow where her head had been. The blood pressure cuff, nasal cannula, and pulse oximeter were just lying on the bed. The heart monitor was turned off, and the IV bag hung from its pole, still three quarters of the way full. *But Lira needs all of that*, Amy thought absurdly. She touched the spot where Lira had been. It still felt warm.

She looked up to see her mother and that asshole doctor standing in the room, looking at her. "Where is she?" she asked, surprised at how small her voice sounded.

The doctor cleared his throat. "She was taken away for autopsy."

Already? Amy thought, but she couldn't get words to come out anymore. Anyway, it was ridiculous. Lira did autopsies on other people. Other people did not do autopsies on her.

The doctor shifted awkwardly, clearly wanting Amy to leave so he could get on with his day. "I'm very sorry, Detective," he said. "She's gone. I can call you a grief counselor—"

"No." Amy slowly sank down onto the empty bed, trying to understand how the person her entire life revolved around could just be gone. She curled up into the tightest ball she could get in and covered her face, trying to shut everyone out.

In that moment, she truly believed she was dying too.

Chapter 16

Amy wasn't really sure why she was still alive, why her body was still functioning. Somehow, her heart kept pumping blood through her body, and her lungs kept sucking in air, even though it seemed like it all should have stopped for her as soon as it stopped for Lira. She didn't know it was possible to survive this kind of pain.

Amy had never lived in a world without Lira before. True, it had taken them thirty years to actually find each other, but Lira had been out there somewhere for as long as Amy had been alive. And once they had found each other, they had quickly become inseparable. She didn't know how to live without her. She didn't want to.

She had been staying with her mother for the past few days, had gotten her mom to bring Henry over here with her. Becky had gone over every day to feed Clea, who would probably have freaked out if they tried to remove her from her home. Amy knew the cat's well-being was extremely important to Lira, but she hadn't been able to bring herself to enter her own home yet. She couldn't stand to be surrounded by Lira's things right now. It would make it seem like Lira was actually there, and Lira wasn't there. She would never be there again. Eventually, Amy would be forced to decide what to do about the house. She could sell it, give away Lira's things, start over somewhere new. But the idea of destroying everything Lira had built over the years seemed unbearable. She could just leave everything as it was and live out her life in that house, assuming she could eventually bring herself to go back in. But the idea of living there without Lira also seemed unbearable.

No matter how she looked at it, the rest of her life seemed unbearable.

Her arms felt frighteningly empty. She could easily remember how Lira had felt in her arms, how readily she fit there, but the actual sensation — Lira's body pressed against hers, her head on Amy's shoulder, her small frame wrapped up in Amy's arms —

111

that was something she would never experience again. She didn't know how to accept that.

She lifted her head just slightly from where she lay, curled up on the couch, when her mother came bustling in the front door carrying a black dress. "You need to get up and shower so you'll be ready for the funeral," Becky told her. "I found you something to wear."

"I'm not going," Amy said, putting her head back down.

"Amy, you can't skip your own wife's funeral."

"Yes I can. I don't want to hear people who didn't even know her that well talk about how wonderful she was."

"Amy, she'd want you to be there."

"Well, she won't know, will she?"

"She might. You don't know that. Maybe she's watching you wallow on the couch right now."

"Well then she'll understand." Amy sat up suddenly, a thought having struck her. "Where even is the funeral?"

"Well you wouldn't take part in the planning, so I turned it over to Lira's mom. She's having the service at Oldham Funeral Home."

"No, that's not what she wanted! She told me what she wanted back when we were still engaged. She was very specific." Their conversation about last wishes came flooding back, and she realized she'd made a horrible mistake by letting Genevieve Ward plan the funeral. At the time, all she had been able to think was that planning the funeral meant accepting that Lira was dead, which she wasn't ready to do. "Shit," she said, rubbing her face. "I fucked up."

"I know you're grieving, but that is no way to talk around your mother," Becky said sharply. She sat down next to Amy and tried to put her arms around her, but Amy squirmed away. "Amy, I'm sorry this is happening, but you're not alone. We *all* loved Lira. We're *all* grieving right now."

"But she was *my* wife." Amy rubbed her face again, hating the question she was about to ask. "What are they doing with her…body?"

"Her mother had her cremated."

"*What?* Lira didn't want to be cremated! She wanted us to be buried together! She wanted Hope Cemetery because it's right by the woods, and she wanted her funeral to be outdoors if the weather allowed it." Amy's shoulders slumped as she realized she had failed her wife in every way possible.

"Well, it's too cold for an outdoor funeral, but we can sprinkle her ashes in the woods. You're the one who gets to keep them. I'll go with you to do it, whenever you're ready. But for now, will you please get cleaned up and get ready for the funeral?"

Amy lay back down. "I'm not going," she insisted. "It's all wrong. It's not even what she wanted."

Becky sighed and walked out of the room. Amy knew she couldn't possibly have given up that easily, so she wasn't surprised when Chief Newman came to the door shortly afterwards.

"Sadler," he said politely, sitting down across from her. "I understand that you're refusing to come to the funeral."

"It's *my* wife's funeral. I don't see why anyone else gives a shit if I go or not."

"I understand that all you want to do right now is let yourself fall apart. I do."

"And now you're going to tell me all about why I can't let myself to that."

"No, I'm not. You can fall apart if you want to later, but you don't have that luxury right now. Today, Martinez, Wheeler, and I will be going to the funeral not just to mourn an outstanding human being, but to keep an eye on everyone in attendance. You know that whoever killed her is likely to be there today, checking out his handiwork, and if he killed her to get to you, then he's going to be particularly interested in watching you. We have a much better chance of catching this guy if you're there."

Amy closed her eyes and drew in her breath, then sat up and pushed herself unsteadily to her feet. "Okay," she said. "I'll go."

***

Amy barely took in a word at the funeral. She was too busy scanning the audience for someone behaving oddly, or for any sign of Hawthorne. He was the one Lira had been most suspicious of, and Amy was inclined to listen to her intuition at this point. Maybe if she'd listened before, Lira would still be alive. He didn't show, however, but someone else did who raised Amy's suspicions: Mitch. Anger bloomed in her chest when she saw him. Why would he come here? He didn't know Lira well enough to mourn her, and he certainly couldn't pretend he came to support Amy. Either he was afraid he would look bad for not coming, or he was here to check out his handiwork. *I'll kill him*, Amy thought fiercely. But she couldn't do anything until the funeral was over.

It didn't even feel like a real funeral to her. It wasn't anything like what Lira had wanted, and anyway, Lira wasn't supposed to be dead. There was no coffin, no evidence that anyone *was* dead; just an urn full of ashes, and those could have come from anywhere. The only sign that this was supposed to be Lira's funeral was that there were pictures of her everywhere.

Amy's breath seemed to stop when she looked at the pictures. It had never really ceased to amaze her that someone as beautiful as Lira could be hers; sometimes, it was hard to believe she was even real. Lira's beauty used to be painful to Amy. It used to be something she could enjoy from a respectable distance, but could never admit to enjoying. Then for two blissful years, Amy had had the privilege of being allowed to tell Lira every day how beautiful she was, of being allowed to stare as much as she wanted, even to touch.

Now Lira was just ashes, and her beauty existed only in pictures. To say it was painful again was an understatement.

When the service was over, Amy tried to just leave, wanting to charge off and find out once and for all who did this to her wife. But her mother dragged her over to a spot beside Genevieve, and she realized she was supposed to stand there and let people offer her their condolences on the way out. As much as every cell in her body was screaming at her to just run away, she stood still and peered into the face of each and every person who claimed to be so very sorry for her loss (as if the word "loss" could even begin to cover it). She searched for some signal that one of them at least knew something, but no one did anything out of the ordinary.

The most distraught person to come through was Dr. Clarissa Hill, Lira's friend and colleague. "I'm going to miss her so much," she said through her tears, holding Amy's hand with both of hers.

"She loved working with you," Amy said quietly. "You didn't...have to do her...autopsy, did you?" Her heart began racing just from having to ask that question.

Clarissa shook her head. "Arthur had her sent to a different county so no one who knew her would have to do it. I haven't gotten the report yet."

Amy nodded, slightly relieved that Clarissa didn't have to go through that. "You'll let me know the results?"

"Of course, I'll call you as soon as I have them. I'm so sorry, Amy. She loved you so much. She talked about you all day every day."

Amy forced a small smile. "She talked about you a lot too."

"I know this is hard," Genevieve told her quietly after Clarissa had walked away sobbing. "But you have to hold it together for Lira."

"Lira isn't here," Amy replied flatly.

"I believe Lira is out there somewhere, and she needs you to find the person who did this to her. She also needs you to take care of everything that matters to her. Her home, her cat, and most of all, her legacy. I raised Lira, but I can't deny that you know the adult Lira better than I do, better than anyone does. You're the one who has to keep her memory alive."

"I'd rather have her than just her memory." Amy looked up at her mother-in-law, thinking of the one secret she had never revealed: the identity of Lira's father. "Lira died without ever knowing where she came from. You never gave that to her."

"Believe me, Amy, I wouldn't have been giving her anything. I'd have been taking something away."

"You always make some kind of mysterious statement like that every time the subject comes up. Lira's not here to protect anymore. Can you at least tell me?"

"I suppose so," said Genevieve hesitantly. "But not now.

Find the person who poisoned her first, and then we'll talk."

Amy nodded. One thing at a time. First she would get justice for Lira, and then she would get answers.

Just then Mitch walked up, and Amy lost all of her composure.

"I'm so sorry," said Mitch, reaching for Amy's hand. Amy wrenched her hand away.

"You're sorry?" she said quietly. "You want me to believe you're sorry? After you gave me all that shit about not inviting you to the wedding and saying what Flynn did to me must have turned me into a lesbian? You don't give a shit about my marriage, my wife. You never even gave a shit about me."

He shook his head. "It's not like that. I—"

"You're probably the one who left that brochure on my desk, who stole my wedding picture and ripped it up!" She could hear her voice getting louder, but she didn't care. "You could be the one who killed her for all I know!" Suddenly she felt herself being pulled away from the confrontation, and she realized her mother and Luis both had hold of her arms. "Luis, I think it was Mitch," she said desperately.

"Okay, but I think you need to get away from here for now," he said gently.

Then she was outside, being pushed into the backseat of Luis's car, and then someone pressed the urn holding what was left of Lira into her hands. Her anger dissipated then, and she dissolved into tears.

Somehow, a smile that could light up a room, glittering green eyes, silky auburn tresses, gentle hands, and the most brilliant mind she'd ever known had been reduced to this.

How could someone who took up so much space in Amy's life fit into such a small container?

"Oh, Amy." Becky got in next to her daughter and wrapped her arms around her. Amy didn't have the strength to pull away this time. She was dimly aware of Luis getting into the driver's seat and the car starting to move.

"I'm a homicide detective," she whispered when her

shuddering sobs had finally started to subside. "But I couldn't keep my own wife from being murdered."

"Amy, it's not your fault," Becky promised. "Lira wouldn't want you blaming yourself."

"We weren't even married a whole year. We were supposed to get old together. We had plans, Mom. We were about to start trying for a baby." She took a shaky breath, the full reality of what she'd lost crashing down on her. "We weren't going to tell anyone we were trying until we were sure it had worked, but we were about to start in vitro. We chose a sperm donor, and they were going to harvest my eggs and implant one in Lira after it was fertilized. Then we were going to use one of her eggs for the next baby, because we wanted two. And then she wanted to buy a bigger house, to raise the children in. She wanted an old house with a big front porch. She wanted to be able to sit in the porch swing with a glass of wine on summer evenings." Amy closed her eyes, picturing the scene clearly. Lira with her wine. Amy sitting with her arm around her. Their two kids playing on the front lawn.

Becky squeezed her daughter. "Lira would have been a great mother."

"She would have been amazing." Amy fingered her wedding band, once a reassuring symbol that she belonged to someone, that someone loved her more than anyone else. "She didn't even die peacefully. I know she was sleeping at the end, but that didn't count. In the last moments when she was actually aware of her surroundings, she was suffering. She had been in pain for hours. She kept crying off and on, and I would get on them about giving her better pain medicine, and they kept saying they'd done all they could. It made me so mad. And then, right at the end, she was so scared. I never really thought she'd be that scared of dying. She's around death all the time, you know?"

"Amy, it's natural to be scared when you're dying. Lira's only human."

"No, I know, I'm not putting her down for being scared. It's just I've seen her in danger before, and she was scared, but not nearly so scared as she was in that hospital. It was like she was afraid of something even worse than dying."

Becky frowned. "What would be worse than dying?"

"I would prefer death to what I'm going through right now."

"Amy." Becky stroked her hair. "That's probably what she was afraid of. She was afraid of how hard her death would be on you, of not being able to take care of you anymore. Which is why you need to take care of yourself."

"She told me not to give up on her. What does that even mean?"

"I don't know, honey. She was sick. Her body was shutting down. She may not have even known what she was saying."

"I should have tried to make it easier on her. She's such a selfless person. Even when she knew she was dying, all she could think about was how it was hurting me. I should have told her I'd be okay, just to put her mind at ease, so she wouldn't have to be so upset. I hate that her last moments were like that. All I could think about was that I couldn't let her die, when I should have just accepted it for her sake. How could she relax and go peacefully when she knew I couldn't even begin to deal with it? She fought it *so hard*."

"Amy, don't beat yourself up. You wanted to believe she would be okay. That's natural. I wanted to believe it too."

A thought suddenly hit Amy as she continued to finger her ring. "Where are Lira's wedding rings? They didn't incinerate them, did they?"

"I wouldn't think so. Maybe they're in the bag of Lira's things that the hospital sent home. I just put it on your kitchen counter and never looked at what was in it. Too many other things going on."

Luis pulled into the driveway, and Amy realized with a start that she was home, at the house she shared with Lira.

"Oh, Luis, she's staying at my house," Becky said as she too realized where they were.

"Oh, sorry, I just assumed," Luis said. "I can take you there."

"No, it's okay," Amy told him. "I needed to come here

sooner or later, check on the cat if nothing else." She slowly got out of the car, cradling Lira's ashes. She wasn't exactly sure what to do with them. She supposed her mother was right, that they should go out and dump them in the woods or someplace meaningful. It was the closest she could get to actually following Lira's last wishes. She hoped Lira could forgive her for this, for everything.

Before she went in, Luis pulled her into his arms, the urn awkwardly sandwiched between them. "I have to get back to work," he told her. "I'll come back tonight."

Amy nodded. "I want you to go. I need you to catch the bastard who did this."

"That's what I'm trying to do. And I promise, I'll look at Mitch. I'll look at anyone who's ever so much as looked at you the wrong way." He gave Amy one last squeeze. "I know this is hitting you the hardest, but we all miss her. She was a really good person."

"She was perfect," Amy insisted. "And this world was never really good enough for her, but...I wanted her to be here anyway."

She walked into her house for the first time since Lira died. It affected her the same way she had feared it would. The smell, the feel of the house instantly hit her, and it seemed impossible that Lira was not there. She could see her so clearly, standing behind the kitchen counter, pouring her tea with a smile. She could also see her sitting on the living room couch with a book, working at her desk in the den, eating at the dining room table. She could see Lira at every point in their relationship: Lira her best friend, Lira her girlfriend, Lira her fiancée, Lira her wife. Lira the mother of her child would never get the chance to exist.

Amy's heart seized. She had no best friend now, no life companion, no future. The best thing she could hope for was that her own death would come soon, so she could be reunited with her love. She would follow Lira anywhere.

She carefully situated the urn on the fireplace and picked up the plastic bag containing Lira's things from the hospital. She begged her mom to let her have a little time alone and, steeling herself, carried the bag upstairs to her bedroom.

Another wave of almost unbearable emotion hit her when

she saw their bed. She could almost see Lira, naked and breathtaking, asleep on her side of the bed with a sweet little smile on her face. Lira's beloved cat Clea was curled up on the pillow in her place, though she stood with a hopeful meow when she saw Amy, no doubt hoping Amy's appearance meant Lira wasn't far behind. Amy's body was wracked with such pain that for a moment she couldn't move, couldn't even breathe. Finally it subsided just enough that she was able to walk to the bed and lightly run her hand over Lira's spot, then pet the poor cat. She took a deep breath and poured the contents of the bag onto the bed.

There was Lira's purse, which Amy had made a point of bringing when she followed the ambulance to the hospital. She would have to go through that later, even though it felt wrong. Lira's purse was supposed to be private. Aside from the that, there was only Lira's book and that purple pen Becky had lent her. No wedding rings. She would have to call Genevieve and ask if she'd gotten them from the funeral home.

She picked up the book. Ralph Waldo Emerson, *The Conduct of Life*. She wondered what could have caused Lira to want this particular book just hours before her death. Becky had said that Lira texted her that morning asking her to bring this specific volume, telling her exactly where to find it in the study, so it must be important somehow.

Amy turned the book over in her hands, inspecting it, and noticed one of the pages had been turned down. That was certainly odd. Lira believed firmly that all civilized people used bookmarks. Once Amy had turned a corner down in a book she had borrowed from Lira, and she thought she'd never hear the end of it.

Amy opened to the marked page and saw a poem entitled "Illusions," with two lines circled in purple ink. Her heart began to pound. If Lira thought turning corners down was wrong, she thought *writing* in books was a serious crime. She wouldn't have done it unless she had a very important message to convey. Amy read the circled passage:

Sleep is not, death is not;

Who seem to die live.

The last line was also underlined: "*Who seem to die live.*" The word "live" was underlined four times. Amy's breath caught in her throat. It was all starting to come together. The funeral that was all wrong. Lira being cremated, and the hospital taking her body away before Amy could see her. The wedding rings that didn't seem to be anywhere. Lira imploring Amy not to give up on her. Newman visiting Lira's hospital room twice in one day and insisting on talking to her alone each time. Lira crying incessantly even though her pain was supposedly being managed. Lira dying the day after she and her doctor had both claimed she was going to be fine. Breathlessly, Amy crept downstairs, carefully dodging her mother, who was impulsively straightening up the house. She figured Newman would have gone straight back to his office from the funeral home, so she slipped out the back door and drove off before her mother could notice she was going.

When she got to the police station, she ignored everyone who greeted her with "Sadler! What are you doing here?" or "I heard about Dr. Ward…" and charged straight to Newman's office. She didn't bother knocking. She just barged in, slamming the door behind her. He looked up in shock, and she fixed him with a glare.

"All right," she demanded. "Where the hell is she?"

Chapter 17

Lira was trying hard not to go crazy. Her funeral was probably over by now, but she still hadn't heard from Chief Newman. She was hoping he would call to say that he'd found a suspect, questioned Hawthorne, or, most importantly, that he'd told Amy the truth. She desperately wanted to know how Amy was doing. More than anything, she wanted to at least talk to her again. She needed to hear her voice.

When Newman had first suggested moving her to a different hospital and allowing her would-be killer to believe he had succeeded, Lira had imagined Amy coming with her. It wouldn't have crossed her mind that he actually intended to separate her from her wife. When he told her it would be necessary for Amy to believe she was dead as well, she was much less willing.

"Since your would-be killer is close to the situation, it's imperative that all reactions to your 'death' be genuine," Newman had said to her.

Lira could feel the blood draining from her face. "You mean you want Amy to actually think I'm dead?"

"It's only temporary. We believe your memorial service could be a good opportunity to potentially spot the perpetrator."

Lira shook her head. "I can't do that to her."

Newman sat forward in his seat, his expression intense. "Dr. Ward, everyone knows how much you mean to Amy. People who barely know either of you comment on the connection you two have. Everyone will expect a strong reaction from her, and anything less could tip the killer off to the fact that you aren't really dead."

"So you want to actually break Amy's heart just to get a big reaction out of her? She would be devastated. I won't do that to her." Lira felt tears welling up just at the thought of it.

Kathy Rhodes, the lady from Internal Affairs, spoke up for the first time. "It's also important to consider that Detective Sadler could *be* the one who poisoned you."

"That's ridiculous," said Lira. "Amy wouldn't hurt me. And anyway, she was upstairs with her colleagues when it happened."

"She could still be behind it," Rhodes insisted. "Perhaps she wasn't working alone."

"For what it's worth, I don't believe Amy had anything to do with this," said Newman. "But it is protocol to investigate the spouse first, and it is my understanding that you are the sole heir to your mother's fortune. If you die, Amy inherits it instead."

"Amy doesn't care about that! She already has access to my money, but she isn't spending it. She doesn't want to." She looked at him, incredulous. "Do you realize she saved my life once, risking her own in the process? She's the only reason I'm alive now! If she were trying to kill me, I don't think she would have rushed over to the morgue as soon as I told her I wasn't feeling well and called an ambulance for me."

"I am aware of her devotion to you, and I know how hard it must be to do this to her. But it's important to remember that as long as you're in danger, she is too. "

"She's in danger regardless," she said evenly. "I believe she is the perpetrator's real target."

Newman held her gaze. "And if that's the case, shouldn't we do everything in our power to catch the perp as quickly as possible?"

Lira's tears began to spill over. "I would do anything to protect her," she said softly. "But I don't know what she'll do if she thinks she's lost me. She's always said she can't live without me. If she believes I've been murdered, I'm afraid she'll do something reckless."

"We'll keep a very close watch on her. Captain Wheeler and Detective Martinez will stay close to her. She'll have family around. I will personally monitor her every move. We won't let her do anything crazy. And just by seeing how people react to reports of your death, we may be able to catch the perp within a few days. Then you can come home, and you and Amy will both be safe. You can get on with your lives."

"You're asking me to destroy her emotionally in the hopes of protecting her physically."

"What would destroy her would be if you really died. This

is the best way to prevent that from happening."

Lira tried to wipe her tears away, but they kept coming. Kathy Rhodes passed her a box of tissues.

"I won't lie to her," Lira whispered.

"I won't make you," promised Newman. "We'll arrange everything with a few trusted members of the hospital staff, and with the police force in the city we move you to. If things go according to plan, we are going to make sure you 'code' tomorrow afternoon. Anyone who's visiting you will be removed from the room, and that will give us a chance to transport you. If you prefer, we can arrange for you to be sedated shortly before then. It might make it easier on you."

"What if they want to see my body?"

"We are preparing answers to any questions your family might have. Let us handle that while you focus on getting well." He stood up. "I'll give you some time to think about it. I'll come back this evening to speak with you more."

"It was very nice to meet you," Kathy Rhodes said as she followed Newman out of the room. Lira just glared at her. There was no chance of a friendship forming there.

When he returned hours later, Lira reluctantly consented to the plan, even though she was terrified of the implications. She realized, though, that it might be the fastest route to catching the person who had been harassing Amy for a few months now, a man who had killed three families in Brookwood and possibly more around the country. Someone who posed a significant threat to her wife. If she had to be 'dead' for a few days in order to catch him, she would do it, but she would hate every second of it.

After she agreed, Newman made arrangements with the hospital to have her heart monitor switched with a training monitor. Once she had been sedated, a nurse would come in to check her vitals and would discreetly flip a switch on the monitor to make an alarm sound, as if she were coding. Amy would be ushered out of the room, and then they would transport Lira out of the hospital and take her by ambulance to the location they had decided upon, although they refused to tell her in advance where it was.

Lira couldn't bear the thought of Amy genuinely believing her to be dead, however, so she found a way to send her a subtle message. Amy was a detective; she knew she was smart enough to decipher the message, if she got it. Lira had to hope she would.

After her transfer she had woken in St. Louis, in one of the best hospitals in the country. This was her home for now. There was a local police officer stationed outside of her room, and most of the medical staff thought her name was Annie Miller. She had never felt so alone in her life.

Newman had sent her a cell phone with his number programmed in. He was the only person from home she was allowed to call. She wasn't even supposed to call her own mother, although Newman had agreed to tell her what was really going on. Lira felt a little ill about clueing in her mother while Amy was left to believe she was dead, but Genevieve's reaction wasn't overly important to the case, she could be trusted to keep a secret, and someone needed to be in charge of "planning" the funeral, someone who knew Lira was alive. She knew Genevieve had been instructed to tell everyone she had her daughter cremated so Amy couldn't ask to view the body. They were going on the assumption that Amy would be in shock, overwhelmed with grief, and would not think twice about letting her mother-in-law handle all the arrangements by herself.

The temptation to call Amy and let her know she was all right was overwhelming. Her heart ached just thinking about what Amy must be going through right now, and she still didn't know if she had made the right choice. Newman was certain that letting everyone think she was dead was the best way to keep both her and Amy safe, but what if he was wrong? If Amy did something reckless and got killed or badly hurt because she believed Lira was dead, Lira would never forgive herself. As it was, she didn't know if Amy would ever forgive her. The only consolation she had was Newman's promise that he would tell Amy exactly what was happening—and put her in touch with Lira—as soon as he determined there was no longer a need for her "genuine reaction."

Hopefully he would decide that soon after her funeral. And, if not, there was still the hope that Amy would find the subtle message Lira had left for her. Newman didn't know about that, but there was really no way Lira was going to leave Amy in this situation without any clue as to what was actually happening. He was out of his mind if he thought she would.

The chelating agent made her feel weak, but she slept fitfully, dreaming constantly of Amy in trouble. She dreamed of Amy throwing herself from a building in an effort to be reunited with her. She dreamed of Amy being poisoned and having no one around to save her. She dreamed once that she went back home and tried to tell Amy she was still alive, but Amy couldn't see or hear her, and Lira realized she actually *was* dead. On the afternoon of her third day in St. Louis, she had a very ordinary dream about waking up in her own bed with Amy by her side, and this dream made her cry harder than any of the others.

She felt vulnerable being in the hospital by herself. It was hard not to think about the last time she'd been hospitalized, almost two years ago now, after her abduction. This at least wasn't as bad as that, but it was impossible to keep the memories from coming up. She needed Amy. Amy had never left her side that last time, and she wouldn't have this time if she hadn't been forced. Amy always made her feel like everything would be okay, her promise of unconditional love wrapping Lira up like a blanket. *Unconditional.* She had to trust that the word was true, that every promise Amy had ever made to her was true, that what she had done to Amy wouldn't change any of that.

The stress of knowing her wife thought she was dead made healing difficult. The previous day, she had been diagnosed with stress-induced cardiac arrhythmia. A nurse, feeling sorry for the woman with no visitors, had allowed her to borrow a tablet, which she'd used to do some of her own research on the case. She'd called Newman with her findings, but hadn't heard back yet. She had moved on to playing Angry Birds when she heard a voice in the hallway saying, "Hey! You can't go in there!" She looked up just in time to see a mass of raven curls ducking under the outstretched arm of the officer stationed outside her room.

"*AMY!*" she cried, ecstatic. Amy abandoned a rolling suitcase in the middle of the room, ran to the bed, and pulled Lira into her arms, holding her like she would never let go.

"Ma'am, you can't come in here," the officer said, flustered. "I'm under strict orders not to allow any visitors."

"No, it's okay!" Lira assured him, unable to wipe the grin off her face as she clung to her wife. "This visitor is always allowed!"

The officer withdrew uncertainly and began to call someone.

Lira kissed Amy's face, kissed it over and over again, running her fingers over Amy's curls to assure herself that she was real. Amy seemed unwilling to let go, and Lira soon realized that she was crying. "My Amy," she said softly. "I'm so sorry for putting you through this."

"Don't be sorry," said Amy. "I know Newman pushed you into it. I'm just glad you're here." She pulled back a little to look at Lira's face, her eyes tracing every feature, her lips slowly curling into a smile. She kissed Lira deeply, then planted kisses all over her face, took Lira's hands and kissed those too. She ran her fingers through Lira's hair and down her back. "You're not as plugged in as before."

Lira shook her head. "I'm doing much better. My heart rhythm is off, but they did an echocardiogram, and they believe it's stress-induced. I'll be fine, now that you're here."

"Newman said there was something weird with your heart that might be stress-related. He didn't want to tell me where you were at first because he's going to get flak from Internal Affairs, since they still see me as a suspect, but then he thought of your heart thing and said you might get better faster if I was with you. Also, I yelled at him. A lot."

"You yelled at your boss?"

"Yeah. Totally cussed him out. He was surprisingly tolerant, though."

"Hopefully he understood your situation." Lira scooted over and patted the bed beside her. Amy climbed in and they put their arms around each other. "So you got my message?"

"Yeah, I found it a few hours ago, and went straight to Newman to make him tell me where you were. I can't believe you defaced a book."

Lira smiled. "I didn't even hesitate. I don't even feel bad about it! I had to let you know I wasn't really dead."

"You're never, ever, ever allowed to die for real. You know that, right?" Amy said, stroking Lira's face.

"I'm going to have to eventually."

"Not before me. I just went through hell believing I had lost you. It's your turn next time. All I want is to die one day before you. That's all I ask."

"Mm, okay. But one day is all you get." She laced her fingers with Amy's. "So they questioned you? I told the Internal Affairs lady it was ridiculous to suspect you, but she didn't listen."

"Yeah, some of the IA people grilled me, but it wasn't so bad. I know the spouse is always the first suspect. I wasn't that upset. I mean, it was hard to be upset about anything else when I thought I'd lost you." Amy smiled, stroking Lira's hair. "But look at you! You're here! You're *breathing*! That is officially my favorite thing that you do." She scooted down and put her head on Lira's chest, listening to her breath and her heartbeat. Lira wrapped her arms tightly around her.

"Have you found out anything about who did this? Newman said he'd question Hawthorne after the funeral, but first he wanted to see if Hawthorne would come to the service."

"He didn't come, but Mitch did." Amy pulled her head back and looked at Lira. "Why is he questioning Hawthorne? I thought he didn't have enough evidence for that."

"He didn't until I did some research." Lira picked up her notes from the nightstand. "Remember how Newman said that one of Hawthorne's relatives was gay? I was thinking, what if it was his sister, the one who died in the fire?"

"Yeah, I thought of that too, but I didn't have time to look into it before we were hit with another murder, and then you were poisoned."

"Well, I did some Googling. A lot of Googling. And I found an article from Amanda Hawthorne's college paper. It was about National Coming Out Day, and she was being interviewed because she volunteered at the school's LGBT resource center. She talked about coming out as a lesbian to her family. She said her parents weren't taking it well because of their religious beliefs, but that her brother was supportive."

"So she's another gay aunt. That could be evidence that whoever killed her also killed our other families, except she doesn't quite fit because she was actually gay and didn't have a husband."

"Exactly, but I had an idea. She stayed with the family while Hawthorne was in Iraq and helped take care of the kids. He came home a few days earlier than planned to surprise his family. What if it wasn't such a pleasant surprise?"

"You mean if he came home and found out his wife and sister had gotten too cozy in his absence?"

"Yes. Maybe he *was* supportive of his gay sister, until he found out she'd stolen his wife away. Then he might have decided to kill the whole family."

"That would explain why he goes after women in heterosexual marriages who are supportive of the LGBT community. Maybe he thinks they're all cheating on their husbands with women, or about to."

"It could certainly have been a trigger for him, to find out he'd been replaced by his sister. So I decided to see if he was currently a member of a church, and I found a link on the Brookwood Believers Church website that mentions him as a church member who helped sponsor a recent youth group trip, which Haley went on. It was for some sort of youth rally, backed by a number of groups that are notoriously anti-gay."

"Brookwood Believers is an evangelical church. They sometimes reach out to the gay community, but ex-members have said they pretend to be supportive at first, with the end goal of basically praying the gay away."

"An odd choice of church for someone who volunteers at an LGBT community center."

"A center that provides people new to town with a list of gay-friendly churches in the area. He had plenty of choices. I'm guessing the OUTpost didn't know what church he belonged to."

"I'm guessing the church didn't know about his volunteer work, unless they believed it was meant as a form of outreach to save gay people from their 'sinful' lifestyles. But perhaps what angered him the most was seeing women who had husbands support the gay community, because he believed it would lead them astray. If his wife and sister did have an affair, then clearly his anger was directed at his wife for betraying him, for betraying their entire family in his eyes, and he may have fallen back on the anti-gay religious beliefs he was raised with. He felt the family was no longer his, that their marriage was a lie. Perhaps he thinks he's saving the men he kills from ever having to find out their wives are lying to them, as he believes they are, because he no longer believes a straight woman can support the gay community. He thinks they're all secretly gay and it's only a matter of time before they betray their husbands. He also kills the children, if there are any, because he thinks they've been tainted as well, but it's harder for him to kill the daughters because they remind him of Haley, his only surviving child."

Amy gave a low whistle. "That's definitely reason enough to question him." She looked back up at her wife and grinned. "Good work, Lira. You might make detective yet."

"I learned from the best," Lira said, grinning back.

"Well we learned a little on our side too. Luis showed pictures of our murder victims around the OUTpost, and people recognized them. Carol Martin's been there a lot to volunteer with their youth group, and Ashley Bibler came in once shortly before she was murdered for some kind of support group or something. Our final victim helped plan the Pride parade, which she marched in with her daughter as part of the local PFLAG chapter."

"So it's very possible that he volunteers there so he can find targets that fit his standards."

"At this point, I would call it likely. What I don't know is why he's zeroed in on me with a completely different agenda."

"I think he wants you. He wants to save you from your 'sinful lifestyle' and make you his new wife, kind of the reverse of his old wife, who married him and then had an affair with a woman. He must have thought killing me would give him a shot with you."

"He wouldn't have a snowball's chance in hell even if you *had* died." Amy smiled at Lira, unable to control her glee at being with her again.

Lira took Amy's head in her hands and kissed her. "I love you so much."

"I love you too." Amy ran a hand down Lira's side and back up again. "And I *may* have told everyone that you were perfect and that you were too good for this world, while I thought you were dead."

Lira laughed.

"But you know what? I meant it."

"Oh Amy." Lira traced Amy's lips with her thumb.

"And I kinda yelled at Mitch that I thought he might have killed you. In that moment, I was convinced he had."

"Well, if he hadn't been such a jerk you wouldn't have accused him."

"Nah, but it wasn't very logical. Doesn't add up the way Hawthorne's story does. I also told my mom that we were about to start in vitro. So, that's not really a secret anymore. She's gonna bug us every step of the way now."

"It's okay. That's a pretty small crime compared to what I did to you."

"Hey, I don't blame you for that. Newman convinced you that it was the only way to keep us both safe. I absolutely blame him, and the IA people, for deciding to put us through all this. I know *you* wanted me to know you were alive. That's why you left that clever little message."

"He said I couldn't tell you at all, in any way, so I had to find a way to tell you without telling you. I knew you'd understand, because you're a good detective." She snuggled in even closer to Amy, not wanting the tiniest bit of space between them right now.

"Does anyone know where you are?"

"Newman knows, but he can't tell anyone, because you're still supposed to be dead. I left Mom a note telling her I needed to get away and promising I wouldn't drive off a cliff or anything. I'm sure she's going nuts, but I had to see you. I *had* to."

"I understand."

"I left my phone behind so I couldn't be traced. I got a bunch of cash from an ATM before I left Brookwood so I wouldn't have to use a card on the road, because then I could be traced, and that might lead people to you."

"How much cash did you get?"

"The most it would let me get was a thousand dollars, so that's what I got. Just to be safe." Amy got up to retrieve the suitcase she'd left in the middle of the floor. "I brought your purse and some clothes for you to change into, for when you're discharged. I also grabbed a couple of your forensic pathology journals, in case you were getting bored." She set the purse and journals on the nightstand.

"Amy. You are the best wife ever."

"You really think so?" Amy got back into bed with Lira, wrapping her arms around her again. "I've been feeling like a failure. I let you get murdered, and I was too upset to plan your funeral, so it ended up being all wrong. It was a big, public affair at a funeral home, and they had you cremated. It was nothing like what you asked for."

"Amy." Lira kissed her wife tenderly. "I wasn't murdered, and I wasn't cremated, and it wasn't my real funeral. And I have my last wishes on file, so in the event of my real death, whoever is in charge of planning will know what to do. It didn't go the way I asked because it wasn't real. They had to pretend to cremate me, or people would have wondered where my body was!"

"Yeah, I get that now. At the time I felt horrible."

Lira kissed her face. "You can feel better now, because you haven't let me down in any way."

Amy closed her eyes, trying to fight off tears, and pulled Lira closer. "My sweet Lira," she murmured. "I'm never going to let go of you again. I'm just going to hold you forever and ever."

"Sounds good to me."

Lira fell asleep in Amy's arms and woke up the next morning to Amy staring at her. Amy smiled when she saw Lira's eyes open. "Good morning, beautiful," she whispered.

Lira wrapped her arms around Amy's neck and kissed her in response. "I'm so glad you found me," she murmured. "And that you're not mad at me. I was so afraid you would be!"

Amy tucked a strand of Lira's hair behind her ear. "I know you didn't want to do this. I don't think I'd ever seen you as upset as you were before they sedated you. At the time I thought you were scared of dying, but now I know you were scared of what you were doing to me. I can't be mad." She kissed Lira's cheek. "Besides, when I thought you were dead, all I could think about was how much I wanted to hold you and talk to you again. Now that I really can, I'm not going to waste my time being angry."

Lira smiled. "How is everyone else doing? Are they upset?"

"Of course they're upset, Lira. I keep telling you, everybody loves you. They're upset about you, and they're worried about me. They'll all be overjoyed when they find out you're alive."

"I wish we could tell them. I don't like making people suffer."

"I know, sweetie. We'll tell them as soon as we're sure it's safe. As much as I hate what happened, Newman is right that the only way to be sure this creep doesn't try to kill you again is to make sure he thinks it worked the first time."

Lira nodded unhappily. "I hope it doesn't take long."

***

A few hours later, Newman finally called with an update. Lira put the phone on speaker. "I've been trying to track down Hawthorne so I can talk to him, but he didn't show up for work today, and apparently his daughter isn't at school either. I sent an officer by his house, but no one was home."

"That's weird," said Amy. "Is there any way he could know we're on to him?"

"I'm not sure who could have tipped him off, but either he

found out somehow or he has other plans. Sadler, you're probably safer where you are. I'll tell your mother I talked to you so she knows you're all right."

"I feel like I just upset everyone for nothing by going into hiding," Lira complained. "It didn't make my killer come forward. We still know nothing."

"You don't have a killer," Amy reminded her. "You're still alive."

"There's a person who *thinks* he's my killer."

"It hasn't been for nothing," Newman promised. "You're safe for now, and you wouldn't be if you were still in Brookwood and everyone knew you were alive."

"I just hope it ends up being worth it."

"I'll call back if we find Hawthorne or if anything else happens," Newman told them. "In the meantime, you two keep staying under the radar."

Amy hung up the phone and looked at Lira. "You know I'm going to have to go back, right?"

"Back to Brookwood? But you're safer here with me!"

Amy touched Lira's hair. "I want to stay with you. I really want to. But I want even more to take you back home and tell everyone you're alive, get you better, and then have a baby with you. And the only way to do all that is to catch the person who made you sick. I know our friends at home are doing everything they can, but I can't just sit around hoping for the best. I have to go help. We need to end this."

"But you're not even allowed to work this case."

"Not officially. But when has that ever stopped me?"

Lira knew there wasn't really any stopping Amy when she was determined. She took Amy's left hand in both of hers, feeling the shape of it, examining the ring that matched her own. "How soon will you leave?"

Amy placed a tender kiss on the top of Lira's head. "I'll stay until they release you from the hospital. I'll be here while you get all the rest of that poison out of your beautiful body, and I definitely want to see that weird heart thing back under control."

Lira felt encouraged. That meant they had at least a few more days together. "When I leave here, I'm going to a safe house. You'll want to know where that is, won't you?"

"Of course! I'll get you settled in there, and then I'll head back to Brookwood to finish up this case, okay? We'll still be able to talk, because you can call me from that phone Newman gave you."

"Okay. But please don't let it take a long time. And don't let him hurt you!"

Amy took both of Lira's hands, lacing their fingers together. "I promise you," she said. "When I find Hawthorne, he is not going to know what hit him."

Chapter 18

Amy opened her eyes and tried to stretch, but she couldn't very easily. Lira was still asleep, lying fully on top of her. It was safe to say she did not want Amy to leave.

Lira had finally been released from the hospital the previous day, her treatment finished and her internal organs still functioning. It would take some time for her to feel completely normal again. Her kidneys had been damaged, but they were recovering, as was her heart. She had survived, and had been far more fortunate than most arsenic poisoning victims. She convinced Amy to stay with her during her first night in the police safe house (well, safe apartment), but now it was morning, and Amy had to go.

Amy savored the feeling of Lira in her arms as long as she could, until both her full bladder and her growing desire to murder Hawthorne became too much to bear. "Lira," she said softly, stroking her wife's hair. Lira stirred a little, opened her eyes, closed them again. "Hey, I know you need your rest, but I have to get ready to go." Lira's eyes flew back open and she lifted her head, looking at Amy with wide, gorgeous green eyes.

I can't leave her, Amy thought impulsively. *How can I go away and not be able to look at this beautiful face all the time? We'll just have to live in this apartment indefinitely.* But then she forced herself to be more logical.

"You have to at least let me get up and pee," she insisted.

"Okay." Lira slowly rolled off of her and sat up in bed, her appearance a little haggard, which was unusual for her even in the mornings. She was still sitting there when Amy came back from the bathroom to get dressed.

"Are you gonna be okay?" Amy asked her gently.

Lira nodded. "I'm okay. I just don't want you to go."

"I know, honey. I don't want to go either. But we both know I have to."

Lira studied her carefully. "I need you to promise me you will stay safe no matter what. When I came to St. Louis, I felt like

I'd lost you. I was completely cut off from you for the first time since my kidnapping almost two years ago, and I was scared you wouldn't want me back even when you found out I was alive. Now that I have you back, I can't lose you again. You have to promise."

"I promise that I will do everything in my power to come back for you in one piece. And we won't be cut off this time, because we can talk on that phone Newman gave you." She gave Lira a kiss. "Now back up a second. You thought I wouldn't want you back?"

"I was afraid you would be too mad that I agreed to this. I knew I was hurting you, but I did it anyway." Lira blinked back tears, and Amy leaned down to kiss her cheek.

"Lira, I know you were just trying to protect me. I know you would never want to hurt me. I can't imagine you ever wanting to hurt anyone."

"And I was afraid if I was gone too long that you would mourn my death and then you wouldn't be able to accept me as a living person again."

"Oh honey, I can't imagine ever *accepting* that you were gone." She sat down on the bed and put her arms around her wife. "There is no way I could have felt anything other than pure ecstasy at realizing you were alive. I mean, yes, I was angry with Newman, but that was because I knew isolating you like this was harmful to you as well as to me." She brushed a tear from Lira's cheek. "I was completely wrecked without you. I kept praying that I would die so I could be with you again. Don't even think for a second that I would ever *choose* to be without you."

Lira nodded and put her face against Amy's shoulder. Amy held her close, realizing even more the emotional toll this whole thing had taken on both of them. And she knew Newman wasn't really the one to blame.

It made her more determined than ever to put an end to the ordeal as quickly as possible.

***

After breakfast, Amy made sure Lira had everything she needed. She had the tablet Amy had purchased for her a few days earlier, she had her purse, and she had most of the cash Amy had gotten before leaving Brookwood. Although the St. Louis Police Department was supposed to provide Lira with anything she needed while she was under their protection, Amy didn't like the idea of her being completely dependent on them. Finally she gave her sweet wife about a million kisses, promised again to be careful, and then hit the road back to Brookwood.

The first thing she did was go home to pet the cat, because she'd promised Lira she would. She felt much lighter this time, promising Clea that her mommy would be home soon. Then she went to her mother's house so Becky could see that she was okay. She didn't want to let Amy leave her sight again, but Amy convinced her that trying to catch Lira's killer was much healthier for her than moping around the house.

"We can go out and sprinkle Lira's ashes in the woods whenever you're ready," Becky said plaintively while Amy got ready to meet Luis.

"Let's get her killer first, Mom," Amy said. "I'm pretty sure that's what Lira would want."

She gave her mother a quick kiss and ran out to her car. She drove to the Elite Diner, where she was meeting Luis for coffee so they could discuss the case off the record. She was just feeding the meter outside when she felt something hit the back of her head, and the world went black.

***

When she came to, at first all she noticed was the splitting pain in the back of her head. She slowly became aware of the fact that she was in a moving vehicle, lying on the floorboard between the front and back seats. She tried to move, but her hands were cuffed behind her. She slowly turned her head to see Haley Hawthorne sitting in the backseat, arms wrapped tightly around her backpack, tears on her face.

I'm sorry, Haley mouthed when she saw Amy looking at her.

Amy turned her head again and saw Haley's father in the driver's seat, which was no surprise. What *was* a surprise was that he was driving *her* car. He was kidnapping her in her own damn car.

"Where," she said slowly, her voice coming out as just a croak at first. "Where are we going?"

"You're awake," remarked Hawthorne pleasantly. "We're going home."

"Where is home?"

"Home is where it all began. Isn't that right, Haley?" Haley just shook her head.

Amy blinked hard, trying to clear her head a little. She had to be on top of her game for this. "You killed my wife, didn't you?"

"I set you free, Amy. That farce of a marriage was keeping you from living a real life. You can have real love now, a real marriage. A family."

"No, see, I don't know what you want with me, but you made a giant mistake by killing Lira. If you'd kept her alive, you could have controlled me. Promise not to hurt her, and I'd have done anything. Now you don't have a bargaining chip. You can't frighten me by threatening to hurt me, because nothing can hurt as much as losing her. And you sure as hell can't control me by threatening to kill me. If I die, I get to be with her again. I don't give a shit."

"I don't think you want to go to Hell, do you, Amy?"

Amy gave a short, cold laugh. "You'll never convince me my wife is in Hell. But I would follow her there if I had to." *I already did, once*, Amy thought, remembering the time she had allowed herself to be kidnapped so she could rescue Lira. Sweet Lira had been dragged into the very pits of Hell that time, and Amy hadn't thought twice about going in after her, so there was really no reason to be afraid of Hawthorne and whatever he had planned. At least she knew Lira was safe this time.

Hawthorne kept his eyes on the road, but she could see his jaw clenching. She looked at Haley, hating the discussion she was going to have to have in front of her, but the kid clearly already knew her father was nuts.

"Why did you set your house on fire?" she asked him.

He was quiet for so long, she began to think he wouldn't

answer.

"That's what I like about you, Amy," he said finally. "You're smart."

"So?"

"My wife," he said, his voice wavering, "ruined our marriage. She turned our entire family into a mockery, a joke."

"Because she was sleeping with your sister."

His face turned deep red. "I was gone for over a year, serving our country. Fighting to make the world a better place for my children. She was upset that I was doing my second tour of duty, leaving her alone with two kids, soon to be three. It was my idea for my sister to come stay with them. She was such a good aunt, I figured she could help out. Make things easier for my wife." He drove in silence for a few minutes. "I got the chance to get on a plane three days earlier than planned, so I could surprise my family. Meet my new baby boy for the first time. I got home, and no one looked happy to see me. They all looked at me like I was crashing their party. I went upstairs to unpack, and my sister's things were in my bedroom, with my wife's things. They were sharing a damn bed. *My* bed. I didn't know my fucking sister was going to take my place while I was gone, trying to take over my wife and kids like they were hers. My baby cried whenever I tried to pick him up, but he would reach his arms out for my sister."

"Well, he didn't know you," Amy pointed out, struggling into a sitting position. "You'd been gone. If you didn't want that to happen, maybe you shouldn't have joined the military."

His right hand jumped out, lightning fast, and grabbed her by the hair, slamming her head against the center console. Then he let go of her and continued like it hadn't happened. She scooted back, out of his reach.

"He would have gotten to know me, but my whole family was poisoned by that sickness, that infidelity. I felt like less than a man. My wife preferred a *woman* to me. My children weren't my own anymore. I set the fire to kill all of us, including myself."

"Daddy, no!" Haley cried.

"I'm sorry, baby, but you're old enough to hear this,"

Hawthorne said roughly.

"So what happened?" Amy asked, casting Haley a sympathetic glance. "Why are you still here?"

"They were supposed to die in their sleep. I was the only one who would suffer. But Haley, she woke up. She started crying for help, calling for me. She was the only one who still loved me. I couldn't listen to her and just do nothing. I couldn't let her burn alive."

Amy looked at Haley. She was bent over her backpack, face hidden, shoulders shaking.

"I had to get her out," Hawthorne said, his voice breaking. "But I couldn't just drop her out the window. She was too small. I had to jump out holding her. So we both survived, and we had to try to make our own life, a life that was real. But I finally realized that in order to do that, our family needs to be complete. She needs a mother. I need a wife."

Amy raised her eyebrows. "And you thought *I* would make a good candidate?"

"When I saw you, I knew you were perfect. You're a very beautiful woman, you know. There's just something about biracial women. You all seem to just take the best qualities from both races."

"I can't even begin to tell you how much we love it when white people tell us that," quipped Amy, flashing her very fakest smile. "My wife always told me I was beautiful, but she made me feel beautiful for just being me."

Amy's head hit the door as the car pulled onto the shoulder without warning. Slamming it into park, Hawthorne undid his seatbelt, leaned between the seats, and grabbed Amy, pulling her towards him. He slapped her, hard, across the face.

"You do not have a wife," he told her between gritted teeth. "Do you understand that?" She nodded, trying to consider if it would be possible to head-butt him while the car was stopped, but he moved away too quickly. "Haley, could you help me move her to the passenger seat, now that she's awake?" he asked, his voice suddenly calm.

Haley reluctantly got out of the car and helped her father

drag Amy out of the back and into the passenger seat, where they buckled her in with her hands securely behind her. Then they both returned to their spots, and Hawthorne pulled back onto the road.

"When Haley said she wanted to interview a female cop for her homework project, I thought that would be the perfect chance to get to know you," he continued, as if nothing had happened. "I thought we would go about things the usual way. We'd talk, I'd ask you out, we'd date for a while. I never meant for it to be like this."

"But then you found out I had Lira."

His jaw visibly clenched again. "You fell for that same trap women all over are falling for now, thinking you can make each other happy and you don't need a man. I tried to get you to understand that. I warned you that I was going to have to kill her if you didn't walk away on your own."

"Actually, you were a little vague with that message." She studied his face, trying to determine if he was entirely beyond reason yet. She decided to try. "What exactly is your plan for me? You can't just kidnap someone and expect her to be your new wife."

"I'm taking you home so you can relearn what a woman is supposed to be. I'm going to show you what it is to be a wife and mother."

"I already *was* a wife. And I was going to be a mother. I mean, if you killed your last wife for turning gay on you, why would you try to make a married lesbian your new wife?"

"The way I see it, I lost her to the homosexual lifestyle, and I didn't have to strength at the time to try to bring her back. I just gave up on her. Now's my chance to atone for that by saving another fallen woman. I believe we're meant to be together, Amy, I really do. I heard that your own father died in a fire. It feels like fate."

Amy rolled her eyes. "Sounds like flawless logic to me."

"I know you don't understand, but you're special, Amy. You'll see, once we're home."

"I'm sure I will. Anyway, where the hell is 'home?'"

"It's the last house my family lived in, down in Belleville. Our home that was despoiled. My wife and I had that place built, you know. It was going to be our home when I left active duty."

"Didn't you burn it down?"

"I had it rebuilt with the insurance money, fixed right back up like it was. Couldn't stand to live there again, but never could bring myself to part with it either, so I've rented it out all these years. I realized I couldn't sell it because I needed to go back there someday, to make things right, when I found a new mom for Haley. She just adores you, don't you, Haley?"

"Mm-hm," Haley said, her voice barely audible.

"We're almost there now," Hawthorne remarked.

Amy watched as they exited the interstate, drove past some box stores of the sort any town had, and then started through the winding streets of a subdivision not unlike the ones their recent murder victims in Brookwood had lived in.

"So why did you kill all those families?" she asked. "I know you killed those other ones, before you moved to Brookwood. If your grudge is against lesbians, why kill straight couples?"

"They were families like mine. Families that were living a lie. Women who cared more about other women than about their husbands or children. Their husbands didn't even know."

"Ashley Bibler was talking to her ex-girlfriend, but she wasn't getting back together with her. Carol Martin was straight. She just sponsored the Gay-Straight Alliance at her school. That doesn't make her gay. The last one, Lisa Stone, she was just supportive of her sister. The gay aunt was her *sister*, not her sister-in-law. She wasn't going to have an affair with her."

For a moment he flinched, and she was certain he hadn't known that information. He had assumed the Stone family was more like his than it actually was. But then he steeled himself and went on. "Once women get exposed to that environment, it poisons their thinking. My wife was straight when I married her."

"I'm betting she wasn't."

His hand lashed out again, striking her. *I've got to start watching my mouth*, she thought. *I promised Lira I'd keep myself safe. She's going to kill me when she finds out I goaded this bastard into kicking my ass.*

"So why did you come to me to tell me you thought the same person who killed these families had killed your family?" she asked him. "I mean, I get it, it's technically true, but were you just trying to throw me off or what?"

He was quiet for a moment. "I wanted you to see the pattern."

"And stop you?"

"Yes." He smiled grimly. "You're the only one who can stop me. Make things right, prove it can be made right, and I won't go after anyone else."

Amy bit her lip, processing. "So that's why…that's why you escalated. Why you killed three families in as many months, why you started adding in those messages. It was because of me."

"Yes. I had to get you to see."

"Is that…is that why you started tying the women to their beds?"

"I knew that would get your attention. The day we first spoke, I had a beer later with your old partner and asked him what you were like. He told me about your attack, how it turned you away from men. How that bitch must have seduced you at your most vulnerable."

"Fucking Mitch," Amy muttered under her breath.

Hawthorne pulled the car into the driveway of a yellow house, drove into the garage, and closed the door behind them. She braced herself as he got out and walked around to her door, hoping to get the chance to kick or head-butt him, but she should have known better. He was a cop. He knew how to handle unruly perps. He guided her from behind, painfully gripping her handcuffs, forcing her to walk into the house. Haley followed at a distance, still carrying her backpack. They walked through the kitchen and down the basement stairs, to a small, unfinished room with no furniture or windows.

"Haley," Hawthorne said sweetly, as he pushed Amy roughly to the floor. "Could you watch her for a moment while I get something?"

Haley shuffled into the room and her father went upstairs.

"Haley, you don't have to do this," Amy said desperately. "If you help me get away, I can get help. You don't have to stay here with him."

Haley shook her head. "He's my dad."

"I know, honey, but your dad is sick. It's not healthy for you to be with him. Do you have other family you can live with?"

She shrugged. "My grandparents on my mom's side are nice, but I haven't seen them in a few years."

"We can find them for you. If you help me, we can both get away, get help for your dad, and get you into a safer environment."

Haley shook her head. "I can't. He'll be mad."

They heard footsteps on the stairs, and Haley stopped talking. Hawthorne came down with a length of rope and held Amy down while Haley wound the rope around Amy's ankles. Amy watched her, silently willing her to leave the rope loose so she could escape, but Haley did as her father wanted and tied the rope securely. Then father and daughter left the room, turning the lights out and locking the door behind them. The room was entirely black now. If she could have put her hand in front of her face, she wouldn't have been able to see it. Once the Hawthornes had retreated, she couldn't hear anything either. *Sensory deprivation*. He was using a torture technique on her, trying to break her. Right now the only sensation she had was the feel of the concrete floor beneath her body.

Amy was scared, there was no point in denying that, but she was not one to simply resign herself to a bad situation. Slowly, uncomfortably, she wriggled until she found a wall. She turned her back to the wall and moved her cuffed hands along it, desperately feeling for something other than smooth concrete, but there was nothing. So she scooted over a few feet and tried again. She knew Hawthorne would have thought of everything, knew it was highly unlikely that she would find a way to get herself out under these circumstances.

But she had to try.

Chapter 19

By late afternoon, Lira was getting very anxious. She had expected Amy to call not long after her meeting with Luis, but she hadn't, and she wasn't answering her phone either. She gave it as much time as she could bear, acknowledging that Amy might just be very busy, and then she called Chief Newman.

"Have you heard from Amy?" she asked as soon as he answered. "She called me when she first got to Brookwood, but I haven't heard from her since, and she's not answering her phone. The last time I tried, it went straight to voicemail, which isn't like her at all. She *never* turns her phone off."

"Becky called me earlier asking the same thing. Amy told her she was going to have coffee with Detective Martinez at the Elite Diner, but she never showed. They think she's driven off again. Martinez is out looking for her; he's afraid she's suicidal."

"Well she's definitely not suicidal, and she isn't just driving around either. I'm afraid something's happened to her."

"Or she found out something about Hawthorne and ran off on her own to deal with him."

"She wouldn't do that. If she knew something, she'd get someone to go with her. She promised me she'd be careful."

"I'll see what I can find out, okay? She's probably fine. She's probably following some lead and doesn't want anyone to know because she's going against orders."

She'd want me *to know*, Lira thought as she hung up.

She paced around her bedroom, the only room in the small apartment where she could get privacy since there was an officer in the living room. Supposing Hawthorne had gotten to Amy, where might he take her? Probably not to his home in Brookwood that everyone knew about, because they'd be too easy to find there. She got out her new tablet and started searching to see if he owned any other property. At first her search was too broad, but then she started to wonder: what had happened to the house he burned down? She did a search for his name and the city of Belleville and found a few articles on the house fire, then one from a few years later about an Air Force pilot. While the article focused on this pilot's happy homecoming, it mentioned that his family was living in a rebuilt house still owned by Hawthorne, with a quick blurb about his tragic story. Lira's heart began pounding. Of course. He wouldn't have been able to let go of the house that easily, not when such a pivotal moment in his life had taken place there.

She hung up and immediately called Newman to tell him her idea for where Amy might be. He did not sound encouraging.

"That may be useful information if we actually determine she's been taken, Dr. Ward, but we still don't know that. Her car isn't at home, or at the Elite Diner, or at the station. It looks like she's driven off somewhere, and it may be ill-advised, but it doesn't mean she's in danger."

"You could just go to the house and check."

"It's at least a four-hour drive, Dr. Ward."

"Couldn't you call the police in Belleville and ask them to go by the house? Just to check?"

"We will if we know there's a good reason. We're not going to make ourselves look foolish to the police department in another city by sending them to a house, most likely occupied by an innocent family, in search of a cop we're not sure we've lost. She's only been MIA for a few hours; my guess is, you'll hear from her soon. You should be resting, Dr. Ward."

Lira was frustrated when she hung up the phone. She didn't know for sure if Amy was in danger or not, and she didn't know if the house in Belleville was where she would be if she were. But she felt strongly that something must be wrong. Amy wouldn't have cut off communication with her. She wanted very much to test her hypothesis about the house, and if no one else was going to check, then she was going to have to do it herself. After all, she was much closer to Belleville. According to Google, it was only about a half hour's drive from St. Louis.

She glanced into the living room. The officer on duty was watching some sort of sporting event on TV and seemed pretty absorbed. She slipped back into the bedroom and looked up the nearest car rental facility. Then she quietly packed what few things she had with her, put on her coat and shoes, and climbed out the window, feeling grateful that the apartment was on the first floor.

She stumbled a little and paused for a moment in the frosty air, trying to get her bearings. She still felt weak from both her poisoning and the chelation therapy. Both poison and medicine had ruined her appetite, so she'd lost weight over the past several days, which also took away some of her strength. She also knew that going on a solo rescue mission was a bit out of her league even in the best of circumstances. But her wife might be in trouble, and it was her job to defend her at all costs. So, with her purse on her arm and her suitcase rolling behind her, she set off on foot to rent a car.

She ran into a little bit of a snag at the car rental place. Apparently, paying for rental cars with cash was just not done, so she finally had to relent and let them put her credit card on file as long as they promised not to run it unless they absolutely had to. The man behind the counter was very confused as to why a person with a perfectly good credit card was so bent on paying with cash, and Lira didn't really want to explain that she was supposed to be dead at the moment. While she waited for everything to be processed, she looked up the house she was going to on her tablet and carefully committed the directions to memory. Finally, her car was ready and she was on her way.

It felt good to be behind the wheel again, actually in control of something after her time in the hospital and in the police safe house. Lira loved driving, but even before her "death," she usually let Amy drive when they were together. Letting Amy take the wheel was a lot easier than listening to her complain about how slow Lira's driving was. Lira didn't actually drive slowly; she always went exactly at the speed limit. It was just that the speed limit wasn't fast enough for Amy.

It wasn't fast enough for Lira either today. Amy had possibly been missing for hours at this point, and there was no telling what Hawthorne was doing to her. Every time her mind ran through the possibilities, Lira found her foot pressing the gas even harder. Thirty minutes after leaving St. Louis, she arrived at the address she'd looked up. She parked her car on the street and got out, realizing she had no plan for what to do next. The sun had been setting when she left St. Louis, and it was now quite dark, but she could see lights on in the house. She couldn't very well just knock on the door and ask him to hand over her wife, however, so she slowly crept around the back of the house to try to get a feel for the situation. She wasn't a cop, so she didn't need a warrant. She was still trespassing, of course, but at least she was trespassing as a civilian.

There was a door with a window in it in the back of the garage, so she went over to look in. There was a very dim light on in the garage, allowing her to just make out the car that was sitting inside. It looked like Amy's car. Her heart started pounding as she squinted, trying to make out the license plate numbers. She couldn't, but she could see a dent on the left side of the bumper that looked exactly like a dent Amy's car had. She decided a cop would consider that to be probable cause.

She tried the door, but it was locked. She looked around desperately for something to break the window with. There was a small shed at the edge of the yard; maybe it would have something. She went over and opened the door. She couldn't see a damn thing, and the crappy little flip phone Newman had given her didn't have a flashlight, but she wasn't giving up. She shuffled along the floor of the shed, feeling with both hands. She found a shovel, but that might be too much. Her feet found a croquet set. That might work, but then she found something better: a golf club. Seizing the club, she hurried back to the garage and broke the window. Carefully she cleared the glass from around the edges before reaching through to unlock the door, and then she was inside.

The door going from the garage to the house was unlocked. No surprise there. She'd autopsied more than one murder victim who had met their demise due to a failure to realize how easy it was to break in through an attached garage. She would have thought a cop might know better, but it was good for her that he didn't. She stepped into a kitchen that looked like it didn't get much use, still clutching the golf club. She stood still for a minute, listening, and faintly heard a man's voice coming from beyond a closed door. She opened the door and started slowly making her way down a flight of stairs into a partially finished basement. The voice was coming from a room to the right of the staircase.

"It's about behavior," she heard him saying. "When you're able to show good behavior, you won't have to stay here in the dark anymore. Eventually, I won't even have to restrain you."

Lira struggled to keep her breathing even. Amy was being restrained in the dark? She reached the bottom of the stairs and saw Amy and Hawthorne through a half-open door. They were in a small, windowless, unfinished room, and both had their backs to her. The light was on for now at least. Amy was lying on the floor with her hands cuffed behind her and her ankles bound with rope, Hawthorne kneeling behind her. Lira had to stop herself from crying out when she noticed blood in Amy's hair. Just as bad was the fact that Hawthorne kept trying to stroke her head almost lovingly. Amy would jerk her head away from him, and he would keep reaching for her anyway.

"Maybe soon," he said, bringing his face down close to hers, "when you're ready, we can make a baby together."

At that remark, all thoughts flew out of Lira's head. In one movement, she pushed the door open, raised the golf club, and brought it down on Hawthorne's head. He crumpled forwards onto Amy, and Lira shoved him onto the floor, not wanting him to touch her wife for another second.

Amy turned her head quickly to see what had happened. *"Lira?!"* she cried in disbelief.

Lira looked down at Hawthorne. He was clearly stunned by the blow, but he was still conscious. He looked up at her, eyes wide like he was seeing a ghost—and he may have thought he was. She raised the club and hit him again, this time aiming for his temple so he would black out. He did. She turned back to Amy, who was gaping at her.

"Look at you, Wonder Woman," she said, her voice hoarse.

"Amy, are you okay?" Lira asked breathlessly, dropping to her knees beside her wife. She could see that Amy's face looked bruised, and it made her furious.

"I'm okay," Amy promised. "But what the hell are you doing here? How did you even find me?"

"I tried to think like a detective. Your phone was off, so I knew something was wrong, but Newman wouldn't listen to me. So I started thinking about where Hawthorne would take you, and I did what you do. I did a search to see if he owned any other property, and I found out he rebuilt this house and rented it out, so I came to see if you were here." She laid the golf club across her knees and began unknotting the rope around Amy's ankles. "What did he do to you? Did he hurt you?"

"Nah. I mean, he did what you just did to him, and he hit me a few times, but nothing serious."

Lira finished removing the rope from Amy's ankles and then helped her into a sitting position before tenderly kissing the bruises forming on her face.

"Haley's here somewhere," Amy said softly. "I'm not entirely sure what her deal is. Do you have your phone? You should call for backup."

Lira quickly pulled her phone from her pocket and called 911, keeping her arm around Amy and her eyes on Hawthorne while talking to the dispatcher.

"The police are on their way," she said when she hung up. Her fingers trailed down Amy's back to where her hands were cuffed. "I wish I had a key for these."

"I'm sure he does," Amy said, nodded her head towards Hawthorne's inert form. Lira started to crawl towards him to search his pockets, but Amy stopped her with a nudge of her shoulder. "I don't really want you that close to him," she said.

Suddenly they heard a scream coming from the staircase. "Daddy!" Haley cried, running to his side. "You killed him!"

"He's not dead," Lira promised. "I just rendered him temporarily unconscious."

Haley looked up and seemed to fully register who she was seeing. "I thought...I thought you died."

"She did. And now she's back to avenge her murder," Amy said drily. "If you had nothing to do with it, you should be safe."

Haley frowned, her hand on her dad's shoulder. "I didn't know he did anything like that until I heard you say it. I kept thinking he would say you were wrong, that he didn't kill anyone, but he admitted to it. I had no idea *he* set the fire at our house." Tears streamed down her face.

"Sometimes the people we love do horrible things without us knowing," Amy said gently. "It doesn't mean you have to be like him."

"I never understood why it was supposed to be wrong," Haley said softly. "Two women being together, I mean. We were happy when my dad was in Iraq. My mom and my aunt were happy together, and they took good care of my brothers and me. I missed my dad, but sometimes I wished he wouldn't come back, because I didn't want my aunt to go away. And then my aunt told me that we would have her no matter what." She looked down at her father. "But then he came back, and I lost everyone else. He's all I have left."

"I understand," said Amy. "And I'm sorry that he has to go to jail now. But there's still time for you to do the right thing. Do you happen to know where the handcuff key is?"

Haley continued to look at her father, as if struggling with herself. Finally she reached into his pocket and withdrew a keyring, handing it to Lira, who quickly located the small key and used it to free Amy's hands. Amy immediately embraced her wife.

"Let's get out of this awful room," she suggested.

***

"So, you told me how you knew I was here, but how did *you* get here?" Amy asked. They were huddled together in the back of an ambulance, legs dangling, a blanket wrapped around them. The quiet street was now awash in the red and blue glow of police lights, a small crowd forming outside of the houses. Hawthorne was handcuffed in a second ambulance, paramedics looking over his head injuries. Local police officers were talking to Haley.

"I rented a car with the cash you gave me. It's right over there." She pointed. "They still made me give them my credit card information, though."

"How did you even get to the car rental place? You were supposed to be under police protection."

Lira shrugged. "I just jumped out a window. I was only on the first floor."

Amy chuckled, giving her an incredulous look. "You never cease to amaze me."

Another car drove up and Luis and Wheeler got out, scanning the crowd for Amy.

"I guess it doesn't need to be a secret anymore that I'm alive," Lira said. She smiled and waved when the men froze in their tracks, staring at her.

"Yeah, sorry," Amy told them. "I couldn't tell you, but Lira's not dead."

"I *could* have died," Lira said apologetically. "But I didn't."

Luis and Wheeler took turns hugging Amy and Lira. "I put a BOLO out on your vehicle when you didn't show up to meet me," Luis told Amy. "After that stunt you pulled, leaving town right after the funeral without telling anyone, I was afraid you were going to do something crazy."

"Everyone was," said Wheeler. "People kept saying they couldn't even picture Amy without Lira. We didn't know what you'd do. Then Chief Newman gave us this address, told us he thought you might have come down here to chase down the person you thought killed your wife, so we took off to find you. We were afraid you'd get yourself killed."

"He did tell you?" Lira asked, surprised. "He didn't seem to believe me when I called him. I *told* him I thought Hawthorne had taken Amy and brought her down here, but he said there was no cause to believe that."

"He didn't say anything about her being kidnapped, but he thought she might be down here," said Wheeler. "We came as fast as we could. Completely shattered the speed limit."

"Did you know all along the Doc was alive?" Luis asked Amy, still looking at Lira in awe.

"Nah. I figured it out after the funeral. That was why I left town, actually. I had to go see her." Amy kissed Lira's cheek. "They had her hidden away in St. Louis. But then tonight she figured out something had happened to me, so she pieced together where I was, ran away from police protection, rented a car, came after me, and took Hawthorne out with a golf club. Which I think is very badass." She put her lips to Lira's ear. "And very hot," she added quietly. Lira grinned.

Wheeler and Luis went to talk to the local cops, and Lira leaned against Amy, feeling exhausted now that her adrenaline rush was wearing off.

"That bastard's lucky it was you with the golf club instead of me," Amy said. "I would have killed him. That asshole tried to kill you, and he was proud of it. If you *were* dead, I'd get in that ambulance now and just brain him. They wouldn't be able to stop me."

"Do you wish I *had* killed him?"

"No. Not at all. You're a doctor. I know you wouldn't feel good about yourself if you killed someone. And, maybe it's better for Haley this way."

Lira watched Haley getting into a police car. "Do you think she'll be okay?" she asked Amy.

Amy thought for a minute. "I really don't know," she said truthfully. "She could go either way. I think she's basically a good kid, and clearly she remembers a time in her life when she was part of a healthy family. Maybe if they get her to a good home, she'll turn out great. Maybe she'll save people, just like she told me she wanted to do. But then again, she's been under the influence of a really fucked-up man for most of her life, and she helped him with kidnapping and restraining me. She didn't seem like she enjoyed it, but still, she did it, and she's going to have that on her head for the rest of her life. She could end up going down a very bad road."

"I hope she'll get the help she needs," said Lira, struggling to hold her eyes open. She felt like she could sleep for days when she finally found a bed.

Amy looked down at her. "You were so not up to doing what you did today."

"But I had to." She smiled at Amy. "You need to go to the hospital and get that head wound checked out. But after that, we can finally go home."

Amy lit up. "Yes! *Home!* And when you're feeling better, we can throw you a big 'welcome back from the dead' party."

Lira giggled. "I'm glad I don't have to be dead anymore. It's the most boring and anxiety-provoking thing I've ever done." She snuggled closer to Amy, wrapping her arms around her. "I wish you hadn't been kidnapped, but since you were, I'm glad *I* got to save *you* for a change."

"Mmm. It's not really for a change. You save me every day."

Lira lifted her head up, puzzled. "From what?"

Amy smiled at her, that special smile she only had for Lira. "From being the person I would have been if I'd never met you."

Epilogue

It took a couple of months for Lira to feel healthy enough to start going through IVF. It took longer than that for Amy to be able to look at her normally again, to just see her as Lira who was always there, and not Lira who she thought she had lost. Everyone had been overjoyed when Lira came back, and Lira seemed continually surprised by the fact that no one was mad at her. Everyone was mad at the situation, of course, and Becky was furious with Amy for not telling her immediately when she realized Lira was alive, but no one had the slightest bit of anger towards Lira. In fact, they all seemed to be going out of their way to let Lira know how much they appreciated her, to compliment her on every little thing.

"I keep telling you," Amy said, "*everybody* loves you."

The third IVF cycle was the one that stuck. Amy had been expecting it to take longer than that, had prepared herself for months and months of egg harvesting and fertilizing and implanting. She had braced herself for the possibility that it would never work, had prepared what she would say to Lira when she decided it was time to stop going down this road. It was a stressful process, to be sure. Amy wasn't wild about the experience of having her eggs harvested, although of course she would have done it as many times as Lira asked her to, and having the transfers done brought up some bad memories, at least for Amy. The first time she had a strong flashback to a day two years earlier, when she had to take Lira to the gynecologist to make sure she was healing right after being raped repeatedly. On the second and third visits, however, Amy was a little more able to focus on the present, and she supposed it would continue to get better as she learned to associate the setting with something more positive.

On the day of the third transfer, the two women had taken the morning off work, and had spontaneously had sex on the living room couch before leaving for the appointment. Lira had told Amy to pretend that was how she was going to get her pregnant, which Amy found amusing; a medical doctor, pretending to do something medically impossible! Once the transfer was completed, Lira made an appointment to get a blood test in two weeks, and they went on with their day as if they hadn't possibly just permanently altered the course of their lives.

Not quite two weeks later, two days before Lira was scheduled to go back to the clinic for her pregnancy test, Amy got a text from her wife: *I need to see you in my office.*

Dropping everything, Amy hurried next door to the morgue, flashing her badge to get past the stepped-up security (though everyone who worked there knew her as Lira's wife), and found Lira waiting in the doorway of her office, twisting her wedding rings. The blinds were closed on the window looking out from her office into the hallway.

"Hey foxy lady," Amy said cheerfully, walking down the hall with her usual swagger.

Lira wordlessly grabbed Amy's hand and pulled her into the office, closing and locking the door behind them.

"Well if I'd known this was a booty call, I'd have freshened up before I came over," Amy remarked, a smile tugging at the corners of her mouth.

"It's not," Lira said, turning to grab something from her desk. She held it up so Amy could see.

Amy's jaw dropped. "Is that a pregnancy test?"

Lira nodded. "I just took it. I was having some possible symptoms, and I didn't want to wait two more days."

Amy stared down at the proffered test, which displaying a little plus sign in the window. Amy knew what that meant. It meant that a *zygote* (as Lira had insisted on calling it) made from one of Amy's eggs had successfully made its home in Lira's uterus. "It's...it's positive," she remarked.

Lira nodded, and a smile began to spread across her face. "I'll still have my blood test at the clinic on Friday, but this is supposed to be ninety-nine percent accurate."

"So you're pregnant."

Lira's smile grew. "Yes, I...yes. It looks like I am."

Amy let out a silent scream, threw her arms around her wife, and lifted her feet off the ground, spinning her around. "Oh, I'm sorry," she said, suddenly alarmed. "Was that a bad thing to do?"

"No, it's fine!"

Amy gently laid a hand over Lira's still-flat abdomen. "There's a baby in there," she said in awe.

"Technically an embryo."

"I thought it was a zygote."

"It was until it implanted. Now it's an embryo." Lira put her hand on top of Amy's. "It's an embryo, with your DNA." She made eye contact with Amy and smiled again.

Amy grinned back, feeling a sudden rush of emotion she hadn't been prepared for. "This is *weird*! It's weirder than I thought it would be. Okay, I'm pretty sure we're supposed to kiss now." She pulled Lira close and kissed her for a long time.

"We can't tell anyone yet," Lira reminded her when they came up for air. "It's still so early. It might not stick around."

"I know. It's just between us for now." Amy hugged her close and kissed the side of her head. "Between the *three* of us."

Lira broke into a grin. "I can't believe it. This is real! I'm having your baby. *Our* baby. We're going to be mothers together!"

"So," Amy said in a low voice, directly into Lira's ear. "I guess that day on the couch worked, huh? I totally got you pregnant."

Lira giggled, stepping back to look at her wife's face. "Yes. You got me pregnant."

In bed that night, Lira happily snuggled up against Amy, who held her close, rhythmically running her fingers through her auburn hair. It was amazing how quickly life could change. The rush of emotion she'd felt upon seeing the positive test had only grown stronger over the past several hours. It was a mix of terror and ecstasy. She had never been happier, ever! The woman she loved was now carrying her child, a little piece of her that would grow into a whole new human being. What could possibly be more amazing?

And yet, she had never been more terrified. They were really having a baby. This wasn't just a game they were playing. There was a new human being coming into existence who would never have been alive at all if it weren't for them. They were responsible for giving this human the best life possible. If this human's life didn't turn out well, even for reasons beyond their control, it was still going to be *their* fault because *they* were the ones who decided a new human should be created in this time and place. That was too much responsibility for anyone! What the hell were they *thinking*?

But no, it really was a good thing. Lira was going to be an incredible mother. Over the months to come, Amy would get to watch her sweet wife get bigger as the baby grew, would see the wonder and amazement on Lira's face when she felt the baby kick for the first time. Together they would prepare their home and their lives for the tiny little person who was coming to live with them, and it would be beautiful. Frighteningly beautiful.

Five months had passed since the horrible experience when she thought she had lost Lira. Little Zoe Stone had come out of her coma and told the story of her attack; although she couldn't positively identify Hawthorne's face, she did recognize his voice. Along with Amy's testimony and Haley's, there was a mountain of evidence against him. He had accepted a plea bargain in order to avoid the federal death penalty and spare his daughter the ordeal of a trial. Haley had gone to live with grandparents on the East Coast, while Zoe Stone would live with her aunt. Amy thought of both girls often.

It was a relief to know Hawthorne was behind bars, to no longer have to worry about threats or being called to the scene of a dead family, but she still vividly remembered the terrible ache of believing Lira was gone, the feeling of her arms being empty. They felt quite full now, with her amazing wife lying in them, and their child inside of her. She had thought it was reckless to love someone as much as she loved Lira, and now there were going to be two people she loved that much. In another few years, if all went well, there would be three. She was definitely past the point of recklessness now, to have so much of her heart in other people's bodies.

But she didn't think she'd want it any other way.

ABOUT THE AUTHOR

Michelle Arnold has been making up stories for as long as she can remember. She graduated from the University of Illinois in 2004 and has been working in special education for the past several years while writing in her spare time. She has published three other novels, *After Raya*, *The World The Way It Should Be*, and *Out of the Shadows (A Detective Amy Sadler Mystery: Book One)*. For her next trick, she'll be working on the third Amy Sadler book, in which she plans to answer the question that has been dogging readers for two books now: just who *is* Lira's father, and why is her mother so secretive?

Ms. Arnold currently resides in Illinois with her cat, Lily Belle. When she's not writing, she can often be found sipping tea while pondering the complexities of Doctor Who.

For more information, follow me on Amazon, Facebook, Goodreads, or Twitter:

www.amazon.com/MichelleArnold
facebook.com/MichelleArnoldbooks
www.goodreads.com/author/show/6489156.Michelle_Arnold
twitter.com/berry2120

Made in the USA
Middletown, DE
20 March 2019